IMMACULATE DECEPTION

A
NOVEL

By:

JACKIE McCONNELL

ESCAPE HATCH PRODUCTIONS LLC

OTHER GREAT WORKS BY JACKIE McCONNELL

TWISTED
PAPER TRAIL
FAMILY MATTERS
UNFORESEEN OCCURRENCE
JOURNEY TO THE BEGINNING
THE PINEAL TREASURES
MY JOURNEY THIS FAR(Autobiography)
PLANT THE SEED
THE PAINTING
PLOTTERS
DEADLY TRADE-OFF
TERMINAL PAY-OFF
BLACK RAVINE
HONEY (CAT)
TWO-FACED
BLACK MAGIC WOMAN(VOODOO CHILD SERIES)
THE LAWYER
RESURRECTION
TATTOO
CROSSROADS
TEEN DRONES
IMMACULATE DECEPTION
SEE NO EVIL
TAKE OUT THE GARBAGE
ROGUE NATION/SPLIT DECISION
THE GIFT
THE CORE VALUE
WHAT ARE THE CHANCES?
TRANSPARENT OASIS

NOTICE

This novel is a work of fiction. Names, characters, places, and incidents either are the product of the author's imagination, or are used fictitiously. Any resemblance to actual persons, living or dead, events or locales are entirely coincidental.

FEDERAL WARNING!

COPYRIGHT © 2020 by JACKIE McCONNELL

PRINTED IN THE UNITED STATES OF AMERICA FOR

ESCAPE HATCH PRODUCTIONS LLC

DEDICATION

This book, like all the other works that came through me, is from the Universal Divine Force. Its purpose is to share enjoyment during these trying times to those that seek and find it therein. It is an honor to be chosen to be the host to deliver this work. The Creator is above all else.

The essence of lying is in deception, not in words.

The Book of Countless Thoughts

1

SAINT HELENA CHURCH
RECTORY ROOM
BEAUFORT COUNTY, SOUTH CAROLINA

Saint Helena Church is an antiquated landmark building that has a rich history. The church was founded in 1712. The building was constructed in 1724, near the Beaufort River. The structure is massive with rectangular symmetry. White stucco bricks were used on its facade. The picturesque church is located amid live oak trees draped in Spanish moss, palms, palmettos, and magnolias. Saint Helena Parish served its community since its beginning in 1712. The building was expanded twice since its construction. First, in 1817, and again in 1841.

During the war between the states, the church was used as a federal hospital. The tombstones in the churchyard were used as operating tables. In the year 1896, a catastrophic hurricane demolished the structure. In the aftermath, it was rebuilt with a beautiful new steeple that was 118 feet tall.

The name Saint Helena was given to the area by the Spaniards who landed there in 1521. Saint Helena, the mother of Constantine the Great, was a Roman Empress in 330 A.D. She converted to Christianity at the age of 63 and subsequently used the imperial riches for charitable deeds and church adornments.

She traveled to the Holy Land to build a Christian church on the site of the crucifixion.

Inside the rectory, stained wooden carvings depicting angelical figures loomed high on the vaulted ceilings. Dark walnut stain color was used as a majority in the interior design. Three men dressed in clerical garments sat in an office with the same interior design as the rectory. One man was a bishop. The other two were priests.

The bishop wore a long, black robe with scarlet red trimmings on the edge of the garment. His headgear was atop the desk. He sat on a high-back, throne chair. The office held gold crosses and figurines. The bishop's name was Arron Wooley. Bishop Wooley, a 67 year old man with flaccid and blotched skin, wore thick eyeglasses against hooded eyelids. The magnification of the lens appeared to enlarge his pupils. Bishop Wooley's experience with church matters went back decades. He had deliberated over some troubling times in the past. Seemingly, it was happening again. The two priests sitting in front of his desk presented a problem that now wasbeing stereotyped into the very fabric of the church.

The bishop ruffled through some documents. The sound of paper crinkling was profound in the quiet, acoustical room.

"Priest Brandon and Priest Conwell these are serious charges, especially with the pressure that is coming from the Cardinals at the Vatican. In the past we could have dealt with these circumstances more discreetly. I am now forced to make a harsh decision. If the complainant were not so well-known and opinionated in the community, I could have probably intervene."

"Sir, I assure you there was no intentions to discredit the church. These allegations are from a great distance in time. I assure you."

"It doesn't matter! Mrs Marteni declares if you two aren't expunged from the parish immediately, she will be forced to go public with molestation charges you two have done to her son. That is something that we cannot afford. May I remind you, Saint Helena Church has a deep-rooted historical past to this region."

"If I may speak," requested Priest Conwell. "If remembered correctly, there were other instances of this nature in the past that were handled discreetly."

"Maybe you didn't hear a word I just said. If this was to go public, the church wouldn't be able to sustain."

Priest Carl Brandon sat still. He studied the bishop's demeanor. What irritated him was the double standard practice being implemented. He remembered being molested by the very man who sat in front of him. Carl was very young at the time. The thought caused anger to ascend within. He felt bile rise in his throat. Priest Brandon was tall, slim, with elongated features. His limbs seemed to be abnormally extended. His aquiline nose, combined with dark circles around his eyes sockets, displayed a mysterious appearance. He and Priest Ted Conwell adorned white, priestly robes.

Priest Carl Brandon and Priest Conwell eyed one another. They communicated without words. Their attention was adverted to the bishop.

"So what do you propose?" asked Priest Brandon. He folded his hands in his lap. Both priests were close in age. The only distinctive difference between the two priests were physical size. Priest Conwell was short and stocky. His clean shaven face exposed early development of a double chin. His neck was seemingly nonexistent because of his broad shoulders. Priest Brandon's brown eyes bore into the bishop's hazel eyes.

"I'm sorry, I have no choice but to relieve the two of you of your positions here at the church. The ruling goes into effect immediately. There's nothing more I can do." He looked away.

Priest Ted Conwell stood abruptly. "I think that's too extreme! Surely you can find other arrangements for us. Maybe you can have us relocated elsewhere."

Priest Brandon became irate as he watched his friend plead against the hypocrisy of the bishop. He quickly stood and approached the desk. "This is wrong!" He reached for the golden cross upon the desk. His anger took control of his emotions. In a smooth fluid motion, Priest Brandon snatched the artifact from the desk. He used the intersecting part of the cross as a handle, and the base of it as a point. He embedded the pointed medal into the neck of the head bishop.

Priest Brandon remained motionless as if he was in a trance. His stared was blank. He didn't seem to hear the question asked by Priest Conwell. His mind was purging ill-emotional feelings that he harbored toward the bishop for years. He reflected on the lengthy amount of time he had to endure the sexual assaults under the bishop's leadership. *'How can you abuse others and pass judgement on them for the very same acts you committed?'*

The bishop sat slumped in his chair with the lustrous metal object protruding from his neck. Blood was only visible on the bishop's neck and fingers where he tried to remove the object before his last breath. His black robe was saturated with a crimson colored liquid. Priest Brandon turned toward Priest Conwell.

"I saved us. They were going to dethrone us from a position that we've endured so much to achieve. This is our church. If we don't run it, no one will."

"I-I don't believe this! What are we gonna do?"

"We finish it!" Priest Brandon removed his blood stained robe. He wore black slacks and a white shirt underneath. He headed out of the office. He stopped at the threshold and turned toward Priest Conwell. Without a word spoken, he continued out of the door.

Priest Conwell looked on bewildered and afraid. Moments after, Priest Brandon reentered the room. He carried a bottle of volitive solvent. He dowsed the bishop with the chemical. He also applied the liquid onto the desk, curtains, and other flammable objects. He struck a match and tossed the flame onto the body. Instantly, flames grew with intensity. The body was now engulfed in fire. Priest Brandon's attention was adverted to Priest Conwell.

"Come on, let's get out of here."

***

Dressed in secular clothing, Ted and Carl entered through a wooden fenced. A wooden gate surrounded the perimeter of a Victorian-styled house. An oak tree stood in the middle of the front yard. Its purpose was to give shade to the occupants. Other homes in the area were spaced apart. The area was quiet.

"Carl, I don't know what you've planned but I am not feeling good about this." The two stood in the front yard.

Carl Brandon touched his friend on the shoulder. He spoke in a low and confident tone. "Easy my friend, I'm just going to talk to her and ask for forgiveness. Why don't you just wait in the car. I won't be long."

Ted Conwell studied his long time friend. He kept envisioning the bishop. The reminiscence caused him to feel unsure and afraid of Carl Brandon. "Okay, hurry up before we're discovered."

Carl waited while Ted headed toward the vehicle. He continued toward the front door. A screen door whined as he opened it to get access to the main wooden door. He glanced at the street activity. He noticed everything seemed quiet. He knocked on the door.

The door was opened by a woman with long auburn hair. Her face was blotched with tiny brownish spots. The woman's blue eyes were lively.

"Yes? May I help…" The door was forcefully pushed inward. The forced sent her onto the beige carpeted floor. Carl entered quickly and closed the door behind.

"W-who are you? What do you want?" It was at that moment she recognized the intruder. "Priest Brandon! What are you suppose to be doing? I'll…" Her sentence was severed at the sight of the weapon Carl displayed.

"Now that I have your undivided attention."

"How can you do this? You are a man of the cloth."

"Used to be. Because of your complaints I'm not anymore."

"You've molested my little boy. I gave all my trust to you. What did you expect I should do?"

"Suck it up! That's what I did when it happened to me. The Lord has forgave me, why can't you?"

Their attention was adverted to the figure coming down the steps from the bedroom. It was Mrs Marteni's son Chad.

"Mom, what's all the commotion about?"

"Run Chad! Run!" shouted Mrs Marteni.

Carl used the barrel of the semi-automatic handgun to strike the woman across the face. The blow rendered her unconscious. A gaping scar was left on her face. Blood trickled down her face onto the carpet. Carl wasted no time, he darted after the boy. Carl Brandon remembered Chad when he was just a toddler. The boy he was in pursuit of was much older. *It's funny how time passes. He have to be at least seventeen now.'* Carl reached the landing. At that moment he heard a bedroom door slam shut. It was the only tell-tale sign of where the boy went. Carl wasted no time knocking. He used his shoulder to gain forced entry. The thin wooden door yield to the force applied by Carl. Splinters of wood flew from where the lock mechanism was once stationary. He saw Chad with one leg out of the window in an attempt to escape. Nervously, Chad turned to the sound of the door as it burst open.

"If you move another inch your mother is dead."

Chad's gaze traveled from the barrel of the weapon to the eyes of his tormentor. His blue eyes bore into Carl's. It was if they were in a contest of who could stare the longest. "Why are you doing this? Don't you think you've caused me enough suffering? To this very day I have nightmares about how you violated my body. I can even smell your rancid odor and feel your sweaty skin on me."

"Step back into the room." Carl pulled back the slide on the automatic weapon. It allowed a projectile to be chambered. The mechanical sound was menacing. The sound was intensified in the small quarters.

"Okay, okay!" Chad followed the order. He stood staring at Carl emotionless. Fear was not an option he considered. Over the years he fought with a deep-seated hatred for the church. He'd thought he controlled what he harbored inside for the priest. For years he wanted to kill him. What he now experienced gave him different thoughts. The feeling to kill was still there; it remained dormant inside of him for years. It was now awaken. Chad closed his hands into a tight fist. Tension he expelled caused his knuckles to turned white from lack of circulation.

"Come on back downstairs. I'm sure your mother want to see you." Chad led the way as Carl followed him with his weapon pointed toward his back.

Chad saw his mother's face as he descended the staircase. He rushed to aid her. "Momma, are you all right?" He inspected the laceration on her face. Witnessing his mother being injured released a rage of anger he never knew existed. Chad's heart rate soared. Pure adrenaline coursed through his veins. He embraced his mother and whispered into her ear. "Don't worry momma, I'll get us out of here."

Carl retrieved a pair plastic zip ties from his jacket pocket. He approached Chad. "Here, put this one on her and the other on yourself." Chad studied the restraints as they were being offered.

HOOONK!

The instant blaring sound of a car horn distracted Carl for a moment. Chad used that space in time to react. He pushed the gun away while holding onto Carl's wrist. They began to wrestle. Chad tried to remove the weapon from Carl's grasp. The match was uneven. Although Chad was much younger, Carl was the strongest. The two fell to the floor rolling and knocking over furniture. Discordant sounds of breakage permeated the room.

Mrs Marteni gazed around for something to use as a weapon to help her son. Near the fireplace was a wrought iron poker. The heavy iron pole held a pointed tip. Mrs Marteni rushed to remove the poker. Chad and the priest continued to wrestle for control of the weapon. Carl held onto the weapon with a tight grip.

A glass coffee table was overturned. The fragile top shattered into hundreds of pieces. The sudden sound startled Mrs Marteni. Carl watched her from his peripheral vision. Energy use from both men quickly became consumed as the struggle continued. Carl mustered all of his strength to position the barrel of the weapon toward his left.

PLOP!

The sound was deafening. It was a thunderous clap, along with a bright flash. The noise overshadowed the struggle in the room. The distinctive stench of gun powder permeated the air space.

A sudden sensation from a hot pinch caused Mrs Marteni to drop the poker. She fell to her knees. Blood from her face, along with the fresh wound to her chest, saturated the carpet. The struggle continued.

Chad noticed what had just taken place. It drained him of all his vitality. He stopped resisting. Chad pushed Carl away as he rushed toward his mother. She was still and breathless. He checked for vital signs. None was found. Chad diverted his attention to Carl. His mind was saturated with anger and vengeance. Carl continued pointing his weapon at him.

"You killed my mother!" Chad's eyes held a distant stare. "Now what do you want? You can't leave me alone like this."

"I'm sorry, it was an accident. I didn't mean to hurt her."

"Too late for that now. She's beyond anymore pain." Chad's facial expression was that of a crazed person. Without warning, he picked up the iron poker his mother once handled. An unsettling scream emitted from him as he charged toward Carl.

"Stop! Don't do that! It doesn't have to be this way."

"You're wrong! You leave me no choice." Chad raised the poker in effort to swing it at Carl. It was raised over his head.
PLOP!

The projectile his it's mark. The noise was loud. The scent of cordite saturated the living room. The stopping power of the weapon was powerful. Chad dropped to the floor in close proximity of his mother. He was dead before he hit the floor. The projectile impacted him at his temple region.

With no time to waste, Carl entered into the kitchen area. He disconnected the gas line from the main valve behind the stove. A hissing sound of pressurized gas enveloped the room. He placed some lead pencils into the microwave. He turned the timer to ninety seconds. Afterward, he hurried out of the house.

"What took you so long? Did she forgive us?" asked Ted Conwell. He was completely oblivious to the past events.

Carl sat behind the steering wheel and drove away. The tires kicked up dry dirt and rocks in its wake. "Yeah, we're forgiven."

SEVEN

YEARS

LATER

2

Ted Conwell was adorned in a white, laboratory smock. He sat at his station transfixed on a research project. He wore transparent safety goggles as he peered into a double lens microscope. Ted was viewing the movement of microorganisms. They were mobile inside a solution on a petri dish. Watching the development caused him to smile triumphal. *'Hmm, nice progression.'* Ted Conwell glanced around his surrounding. He saw others dressed in similar garbs working on different research projects. His job description title was research technician for a giant pharmaceutical company. His division was located in Brooklyn, New York. He took off his goggles and began to rub the tiredness from his eyes. *'I think I'll take a lunch break.'* He headed toward the exit.

The break lounge was lavishly constructed and decorated. Cloth covered tables matched the carpet's color. Food was prepared by professional chefs. The chef's attire included tall, white, floppy hats. An open kitchen was built around stainless steel. Although the establishment was self-service, the amenities were that of high quality restaurants.

Ted ordered a meal and walked toward a table in the rear. He positioned himself near a large, tinted window. The view was spectacular. The high elevation displayed a breathtaking view. The eatery was located on the 25th floor. Ted's meal consisted of thinly sliced strips of seasoned beef on a bed of rice pilaf. Pineapples and celery garnished the sides of the square plate. A pitcher of ice tea was placed on the table. Ted delightfully ate his food. What brought him the most joy was the results of the test.

Ten minutes into the meal, his mind wandered aimlessly. He thought of Carl Brandon. It had been years since the two separated. He remembered when they parted at the airport. Carl handed him an envelope. His eyes widened as he inspected the content. The envelope contained a bundle of 100 dollar bills.

As he rode on the Greyhound bus, it darned on him as to where Carl obtained the cash. Ted remembered Carl taking time to return from a room in the rectory. He recollected Carl returning with a canister of solvent. He noticed something protruding from his waist. It was hidden beneath his shirt. *'Although we did do wrong, he is my friend. I'm still asking for forgiveness.'* Ted was jolted back from his reverie by an attractive female researcher. She worked in his department. She held a tray in her hand.

"Do you mind if I join you?" asked the woman. Her bluish-green eyes mesmerized him.

"Sure, it would be my pleasure." He studied her demeanor as she sat. Although she was adorned in an identical lab coat as his, he was able to see her slender curvaceous figure silhouette through the thin fabric. Her hair was sandy brown. It matched her eyebrows perfectly. *'A natural.'* Ted had been attracted to her from the first day they met. It was an ill-feeling for him because he could not remember being attracted to the opposite sex so strongly.

"Miss Houghton…"

She held up a protesting hand. "Call me Adrianna. We're colleagues. Plus, I want to thank you for the advice you offered with the sound waves and bacteria theory. Who would have thought the two forces would have conflicting properties when introduced together? The fact that different magnetic charges were created is amazing."

Ted raised his hand jokingly. "I did…"

"That you did." Adrianna smiled. She exposed perfectly, pearly white teeth. Her lips were small. Ted noticed her eye sockets were downturn in shape. "Tell me, what are you working on now?" She spooned food into her mouth.

Ted fought hard not to stare. "Well, I am working on a contraceptive. When I am finish, I will have it delivered through an atomizer."

"I'm impressed." Adrianna spooned some cream of asparagus soup into her mouth. She dabbed at her lips with a napkin. "I notice you don't talk much or socialize with the others. Do you have a girlfriend?"

Ted was sipping on a beverage when she asked the question. The straightforwardness of her question caused him to choke on the liquid as it passed through the wrong tube. He made guttural cough sounds to clear his throat.

"Are you all right?"

"Sure, excuse me…" Ted regained his composure. "I'm sorry, it was the combination of the liquid and the frankness of your question that caught me off guard." Adrianna smiled. "The answer to your question is no. I don't have a girlfriend."

Feeling slightly embarrassed, Adrianna broke her stare. "I-I didn't mean to be so inquisitive. It's something that I'm struggling with. You see, as a young girl my mother said I had so many questions. I guess it is why I'm a research technician."

"Please, don't feel bad. I find it charming that you can say what you think."

"What is it that you think?"

'Another unguarded question.' He sighed deeply. "I think you're a very attractive woman. Your character is vibrant."

"That's cute, I've never been described as such before."

"I know this is our livelihood and I wouldn't want to do anything that could jeopardize that. It's the only reason that I keep my distance."

"That's honest of you." She gazed at her watch. "Well, it was nice chatting with you. I have to be getting back to the laboratory. You know they can't function completely without me." She smiled.

"Thank you for the visit." He watched as Adrianna stood and departed. Her strides were sensual. He continued to watch. He observed the way her hips swayed as she walked. The mere thought of possessing her excited him. Boyish thoughts controlled his emotions. *'Easy boy.'* Ted Conwell never experienced intimacy with a woman. After the many sexual encounters with Bishop Wooley, he was left feeling impotent and confused. The deep psychological scar he carried was indescribable. There were no words that could be uttered that related to the emotional pain he endured. *'It has been a lot of years and I really do like Adrianna.'* Ted's mind was experiencing a dilemma. The only time he could feel an erection was when he was in the company of young boys. He fought hard to correct his wrongs and not give into the urges.

3

"Father I have sinned," stated Carl Brandon. He sat inside of a confessional at Saint Martin's church. The locating was in Memphis, Tennessee. A hand carved mesh screen partitioned the compartment from the another other side. A silhouette of a figure could be seen through the screen.

Father Mahoney sat in his enclosure dressed in a priestly robe. He was an elderly man that had been with the parish for two decades. His voice held a southern twang. "When was your last confession?"

Being in a juxtaposed position, Carl was positioned slightly facing the screen on his side of the enclosure. His view was also a silhouette. "It has been some time but my repentance is great."

"What would you like to confess my son?"

"That I've betrayed a cardinal rule. I've murdered multiple persons. It was not done out of joy, but necessity."

Father Mahoney listened on startlingly. His experience over the years listening to confessions, he'd heard diverse stories. Some similar to the one being told to him. What troubled Father Mahoney was the way the parishioner spoke. He sounded convinced he had the power to give and take life righteously. It was quite disturbing to the priest. "Do you mean as in the act of war? As a service to your country? The armed forces maybe?"

"No."

"Would you like to elaborate more?"

"I want to have it confirmed I am in accordance with the will of God. Having you listen confirms my mission."

"Your mission you say? What might that be?" Father Mahoney became unsettled.

"To lead my own flock once again. To bring them closer to God than any of the clergies before me ever could."

"Have you spoke to the authorities on this matter?"

"For what?" snapped Carl. "We are the authorities on earth. The secular population is not in control. You should know that." The pitch of his voice rose with excitement. "I've said enough!" Carl quickly stood and exited the confessional. He blended in with the other parishioners. He made his way toward the main exit.

Father Mahoney tried to move swiftly to get a direct identification of the confessor, but his physical impairment made that impossible. By the time he exited the confessional, the person he'd encountered was already gone. Troubled by the conversation, Father Mahoney headed toward the alter to pray for the individual. He grieved for all the misfortunate people that will cross paths with the confessor.

***

Carl Brandon turned off the shower. The spray of icy water felt rewarding as it pricked his skin. He felt vigorous as he dried his body in front of a full-length mirror. He studied his reflection. His nudity revealed self-inflicted scars and burns. His pale complexion was contrasted by bruises and lacerations. *'You must continue to repent.'* He walked toward a counter that held towels and soaps. He retrieved a brown chamois material. Unrolling the leather satchel revealed what appeared to be surgical tools. The items included scalpel, forceps, and an extractor. The stainless-steel tools gleamed in the presence of the bathroom lighting.

Picking up the scalpel, he studied its honed edge. Using the scalpel, Carl began making superficial incision upon his skin. The symmetrical patterns resembled that of a cross in the middle of his chest. Blood cascaded onto the ceramic tile floor. *'Yes! Forgive me father for what I have done, and for what I'm about to do.'* Dark, sinister laughter filled the small enclosure. When the merriment subsided, Carl Brandon opened a plastic bottle of isopropyl alcohol. He poured the liquid content onto the fresh open wounds. A cold sensation from the temperature of the alcohol quickly dissipated into an agonizing burning pain. Carl welcome the sensation. He felt the dissimilar sensations and associated it with good and evil. In his cloudy, confused cognizance, he was withstanding the torment of the world upon his shoulders. In Carl's mind, he was giving God a much needed rest. Tight lipped, he withstood the excruciating pain. As the pain subsided, Carl dabbed more of the alcohol onto his left forearm with a cotton ball. He lit the solution with a match. The highly volatile and flammable liquid caught aflame. The solution began to heat as the pain began to intensify. When the alcohol was completely evaporated, the flame extinguished. The results left red, discolored skin tissue. Carl's tightly closed lips and teeth wanted to open and release the inward pain, but he withstood it for the world. He stopped into the shower stall to wash away the world's sins once again. Dressed in clerical garbs, Carl Brandon exited the house.

Carl remembered the time of his separation from Ted. He remember sharing the pilfered cash with him. Carl used his portion of the proceeds to purchase a used vehicle. He discovered Ted pursued another field altogether in New York City. Carl decided to head toward Yonkers. It was a town located in Westchester County, New York.

A predetermined plan was set into motion. His first stop was the county register office. Carl located a dilapidated building just 45 minutes from New York City. Using false identification, he purchased the building and registered it as a church. After spending three years on the project, it was finally completed. The building was christened, ALL SAINTS CHURCH. The exterior of the building was designed handsomely. White frame windows decorated the facade. The interior was designed and decorated with style and class. Beautiful wood carved pews and kneeling platforms were constructed. A three-decker wineglass pulpit was erected in the church. Soon after, donations began pouring in when the church went online. Local residences began donating their skills and time to build the church to high standards. Word began to travel fast about the church. Volunteer nuns and other cleric personnel joined in the movement to help.

There was a common bond in the air. Everyone felt the church was divinely sent and needed. Carl, now known as Priest Hamilton, had his own flock.

After the business of running the church, Carl witnessed that changing his sir name wasn't enough to ensure success. Another problem persisted. The church was not generating enough money to stay afloat. The cash flow on hand was steadily declining. *'I must enlarge the flock. There has to be a way to create a buzz like the big boys do.'* An idea occurred. It was time to talk to Ted.

4

Sister Beatrice was in class working with third grade children. The students were word building with the use of plastic letter blocks. The strategical lesson was in the form of a contest game. The rules were whosoever made the largest word, and knew its meaning, would be the winner for the day. Winner or not, everyone would receive an ice cream cone at the end of the session. Sister Beatrice loved the children and they in turned showed deep reverence for her. At times she would use her own meager earnings to purchase learning material for the children.

Sister Beatrice's mother was also a nun at a convent in Lafayette, Louisiana. She gave birth to Beatrice before becoming a nun. Beatrice was raised in the faith. It's the only life she'd ever known. Beatrice's mother died when she was 17. It was then she decided to explore the world. Her first thought was to volunteer her services internationally. She decided to join the Red Cross. Three years prior, she heard about a new parish being assembled online by volunteers and donations. Since she didn't have any worldly possessions, she decided to volunteer her services at that location.

After meeting Priest Hamilton, she was all too happy to participate. There were plenty of young men helping out with their skilled labor and services. Although she'd never been with a boy, she never felt inquisitive to do so. Keeping her virginity wasn't even a second thought to her. The children were a way for her to cope with uncertain feelings that arose from within.

Sister Beatrice sat in the office of Priest Carl Hamilton. Both were dressed in their clerical garbs. Beatrice's light blue eyes bore into the priest's eyes. She used her fingers to remove her sandy brown hair from blocking her view.

"We need new books for the children. They're outgrowing the current ones. The supplies from donations is dwindling fast."

"Sister Beatrice…" Priest Hamilton folded his hands atop the desk. "I am quite aware of our current financial crisis. I am making every effort to correct the situation."

"I'm sorry, I didn't mean to…"

Carl held up a hand in protest. "Nonsense! You are just displaying genuine concern." He stood to gesture that the meeting had come to an end. Sister Beatrice followed suit. She stood facing the priest. "If you'll excuse me, I have another appointment to attend."

"Sure Father." Sister Beatrice headed out of the door.

Later that day, Sister Beatrice walked up and down the busy main street handing out flyers for an upcoming bake sale. A few of the nuns decided to take matters into their own hands. Their efforts was to bring the desperately needed funds into the church.

The local pedestrian traffic was friendly to the nuns. Many stopped to socialize with them. Sister Beatrice's reputation for caring was astounding. Many times, she would charter the children on field trips the church struggled to support. Many of the children were orphans and wards of the state. The church relieved the crowded system of as many children as they could afford.

***

The evening sky opened to a dark, grayish-blue hue. Cumulus clouds formed in the nocturnal ethers. Sister Beatrice was heading back to the parish with a shopping bag filled with pencils, composition notebooks, and plastic pencil sharpeners.

As she crossed the avenue, a black cargo van intercepted her path. The cargo door slid open. Two figures exited the vehicle and accosted Sister Beatrice. They wore dark clothing and adorned nylon stockings over their heads. The coverings distorted their facial features. She tried to scream as the packages she held fell to the ground. The sound of her scream was short lived. One of the abductors placed a chemically laced material over her nose and mouth. A sweet, pungent odor filled her nostrils as she struggled to breathe. Within seconds, Sister Beatrice stopped resisting. Her body went limp in the arms of the kidnappers. She was ushered into the van. The tires screeched as the vehicle picked up momentum and traction. The only tale-tale sign left at the scene were the spillage of stationary supplies from the packages she once carried. The school supplies were scattered on the street.

Ted Conwell exited his brownstone studio apartment. It was located in the Canarsie section of Brooklyn. He headed toward his vehicle when a cargo van came to a full stop directly in front of him. Two men quickly exited the vehicle and rushed toward him. Ted's first thought was police officers. As if rehearsed, the men moved methodically to subdue Ted. One of the abductors restrained his arms while the second man forcefully placed a chemically soaked material over his nostrils. Almost instantaneously, Ted went limp in the captor's arms. He was carried to the van and driven away. The abduction was done so systematically, it went unnoticed by anyone on the residential block.

Large colorful flamingo birds flapped endlessly along the Great Lake. Some birds dived for fish. Bright sunlight intensified as droplets of water touched his face. A slight pinch jolted him. Ted Conwell was awakened from his drug induced stupor. He opened his eyes to blurred sight. A hazy figure loomed over him. He strained to focus. A bright light hovered, adding to his impaired vision. Sprinkles of cold water masked his face. Moments passed before Ted's equilibrium was restored. His mind raced to recollect his whereabouts. He remembered leaving the house and heading toward his vehicle. Ted's eyes became sharp with clarity. The figure in front of him caused him uncertainty. Momentarily, he thought he was dreaming.

"Carl? Is that really you?"

Carl reached out a hand. He helped Ted to sit upright. Ted gazed around at the unfamiliar setting. The place resembled an emergency room in a hospital. Stainless-steel tables, desks, and lights were part of the room's decor. Stainless-steel cabinets held pharmaceutical supplies.

"Yes it's me." His face gleamed from happiness at seeing his friend.

"W-what is this place? Why am I here?"

"Easy old friend, everything is fine. I'll answer all of your questions, but first let me get you something to drink."

Ted's dry throat was the aftereffect of the chlorophyll. A sweet, pungent aroma still existed in his mouth and nostrils. "Why was I abducted and brought here?"

"Here, drink this…" Carl handed Ted an unopened bottle of spring water. He took a seat opposite from where Ted sat. "This place is a rental laboratory. It has state-of-the-art equipment if I may say so…" He gestured with his hands to display the room. "I need for you to do a small operation on a patient."

"Operation?" Ted was bewildered.

"Yes, we will get to that. First, I want to apologize for the manor I use to invite my long time friend. I've been keeping tabs on you. I'm proud of what you've accomplished with your career."

"What do any of this has to do with me?"

"I now have my own church, only it isn't generating enough donations to keep it afloat. I know your studies include reproduction and contraceptives."

Ted studied Carl's demeanor. "Are you feeling all right?"

"Now that you're here, things couldn't be better." His laugh was cynical. "Here's what I want you to do…"

6

Yonker County Police were converged at the scene of the All Saints Church. Clergy members were being questioned by police officers in efforts to find answers to the mysterious disappearance of Sister Beatrice.

A tall, slim man of African-American descent entered the room. He was dressed in a stylish, ash-gray suit and a charcoal colored tie. He also adorned an egg-white shirt. He sported transitional eyewear that began to lighten as the moments passed. His complexion was soft brown. His face was clean shaven, except for a well trimmed goatee. He entered the room displaying his badge. He approached Priest Hamilton.

"My name is Detective Hall. I need to know who saw…" He was lost for words because he didn't remember the name of the victim.

"Sister Beatrice, she's a third grade school teacher here at the parish. Everyone loves her. I don't know anyone that would harm her."

"Who saw her last?"

"She filled out a voucher to get school supplies. We deal with the local stationary store on Main Street."

Detective Hall entered the local stationary store. The establishment was moderately sized with long aisles filled with assorted items. Customers shopped with the use of hand held baskets. Detective Hall headed toward the counter. An elderly woman with blonde hair, hazel eyes, and rosy cheeks had just finished serving a customer. Her service name tag read BETTY.

"Hi, my name is Detective Hall…" He displayed his badge. "I would like to talk with the manager. Is he in?"

Her voice was high-pitched with a twangy accent. "Yes, I'll call him." She reach for the telephone.

"Wait! Before you do, I want to ask you a few questions."

Betty removed her hand from the receiver. "Why sure."

"Do you know of a nun by the name…" He referred to his notepad. "Sister Beatrice?"

"Sister Beatrice? Who doesn't? She's the finest example of humanity amongst young people we have. She teaches the third graders at the parish. Why do you ask? Is something wrong?"

"I just need to know when was the last time you've seen her?"

"Just earlier, she came in as she always does from time to time to purchase supplies for the children. I'll tell you one thing, she was the purest this town has."

"I don't understand."

"Some say she was born in the church and has never been touched. Do you understand now?"

Detective Hall nodded. "Yes." He studied his notes again. "Do you remember what she purchased?"

Betty thought for a moment. "I can do better than that." She reached into a drawer. "Here's a copy of her receipt."

"Can I keep this?"

"Sure." Betty saw the detective heading for the exit. "I thought that you wanted to talk to the manager."

"I think I have enough information." Detective Hall headed through the threshold.

"You didn't tell me if she's all right?" The detective continued onward.

Detective Hall tried to retrace Sister Beatrice's possible path. He noticed the streets were narrow and quiet. Shops on both sides of the street were open for business. Detective Hall kept a keen eye on the sidewalk as he looked for clues. He headed across the street toward the corner. He stopped. Detective Hall picked up a few packages of pencils. They were on the southeast part of the street. He searched on further. Next to a parked vehicle he spotted a shopping bag with a store logo on front. Inside was notebooks and erasers. They were still in their original packaging. It indicated that they were dropped suddenly. He placed the bag down. Another detail captured his attention. He noticed tire tracks. Black rubber burned into the asphalt from sudden acceleration. He used his cellphone to take photos of the markings. With that done, he dialed a number.

"Yeah, it's me Sandy. I'm sending you a few photographs. I need a profile data sheet on them. Thank you." He disconnected the connection and headed back toward the church.

Detective Hall was stopped by a short stature woman. She wore a brown, leather jacket. She stepped in front of his path.

"Are you a police officer?"

"Yes." Detective Hall displayed his badge. "I'm a detective. Can I help you?"

"Is your investigation about Sister Beatrice?" Detective Hall was caught off guard. He nodded. "I saw a black cargo van appear just as Sister Beatrice was crossing the street. She was carrying a plastic shopping bag. The van blocked my view. When it drove away, Sister Beatrice was no longer there. I was afraid and didn't want to be involved. I managed to call you guys."

"You've done the right thing." He jotted down her information. What is your name?"

"Is that necessary? As I said, I don't want to be involved. I work in the book store over there…" She pointed across the street.

"Okay, of course. I understand." Detective Hall put away his notepad. "I'll call if I have anymore question. Thank you for showing concern."

"Thank you, I hope she's safe."

"So do I."

7

With an armed security guard in the hallway, Ted Conwell experienced an unfit rest. His mind continued to wander. He tried to understand what was unfolding. *'Carl is acting so strange. Maybe I better do what he wants and get out of here. Maybe then I can notify the authorities.'* Ted gazed around at the windowless room. It was impossible to know if it was day or night. A knock came to the door. It was opened by Carl.

"Hey, let's get something to eat before we get down to business." Carl led him to a small kitchen. Food was already prepared on the table. The two men sat next to hot, steaming plates of food. Carl said grace while Ted looked on uneasily with his head bowed.

Ted watched Carl take a forkful of food and place it into his mouth. "You still haven't told me who or what this operation is about. I am a medical science technician, not a surgical doctor."

Carl placed his fork down. He took a sip of water to wash down the food in his mouth. "I'm very much aware of what you do. What I am asking is simplistic in nature. I need for you to implant semen into a woman, adjacent to her uterus. The sperm must be contained and suspended. It will be in a time release sac that will eventually drop into the fallopian tubes during ovulation."

Ted studied Carl's face questionably. "That's absurd! I've never heard of anything so...so preposterous."

"No..." Carl held up his hand in protest. "I've studied the matter in its entirety. It can work. Using DNA sampling, I've received information of her menstrual cycle. The key is we use a foreign biochemical matter as the cache. The body's natural defenses will attack the intruder. If her immune system is intact, it will began to dissolve the matter over a period of time, releasing the cells into the tubes."

Ted held a bewildered expression. "But won't that cause pregnancy?"

Carl smiled. "Yes, that is the intended effect."

"But why?"

"That's not important. Let's go get prepped for the job ahead."

"What if I refused?"

Carl's smile was cynical. "Remember, we have a history together." He gave Ted a sly wink of the eye.

***

Ted was allowed to wash and change into surgical scrubs. He now adorned a lime green hat with matching top and bottom. Ted was escorted into another sterilized environment. The layout was similar to the first, only the room he occupied held an unconscious body on the operation table.

Ted apprehensively approached the table. Carl was wearing identical clothing. He stood by Ted's side. Ted noticed the woman's vital signs were being monitored by graph machines. Ted turned toward Carl.

"Really? What is this all about? Carl what are you mixed up in?"

"I told you. All you have to do is insert what I asked of you and we're set. The church is set."

"But we don't know if it will work." Ted looked to the woman. His gaze returned to Carl.

"I'll take my chances. Now let's get started."

Ted eyed the tools he would need. They were lined aside the table. He noticed the items were sterilized. The woman was naked. Ted couldn't help but to notice the woman was beautiful and her physique was stunning. *'She's young, what's going on here?'* He examined the woman's vagina to see if she had been recently penetrated. Suddenly, a strange sensation entered his body from his core. He shrugged it off and continued. He knew deep inside his cognizance it could be worst. He realized he was dealing with a mentally unstable person. Upon further inspection, Ted came to the conclusion that the woman on the table was a virgin. That evaluation was confirmed from viewing her intact hymen. The thin membrane was still partly closed over the vaginal opening. *'What is going on here?'* Ted picked up a nontoxic vegetable paste pen and drew an outline at the region of her ovaries. Using a fiber optic camera, a tool used to pinpoint the exterior positioning, Ted began the tedious work ahead. Sweat began to swell on his brow. Carl, stood next to him and dabbed at Ted's forehead with a cloth.

After two hours of intense concentration, the operation was finally over. Ted was able to attach an artificial insemination device directly atop the ovaries. The device held two hollow tubings that intruded directly into the ovaries. Upon dissolving, the semen would be directed into the ovaries. It would then travel along the fallopian tube toward the uterus. If everything went according to plan. The planned pregnancy will seem like the biblical birth of Jesus Christ and the Immaculate Conception.

Ted Conwell reported to work the next morning. After passing through the decontamination area, he headed into the laboratory. He sat at his station reviewing the data from the previous days. Adrianna approached his station. Ted looked up from his dual lens microscope. Adrianna's beautiful smile and sensual lips caused his heart to feel heavenly. Seductive thoughts plagued his mind.

"Hi, how's it going?" She remained standing over him.

"The data is checking out to be accurate." Ted removed his clear safety goggles to stare into her livid, bluish-green eyes. "I should be ready to give it a final diagnostic before trying it out."

"That is so exciting. Let's celebrate!" Her eyes gleamed.

"In my department that may be a bit premature." He smirked.

Adrianna chuckled at the antic. "I guess I deserved that. But for real, let me take you out to dinner tonight?"

"Are you asking me out on a date?"

Adrianna thought for a moment. "I guess I am. Yes, it's a date." She blushed.

"Okay, we can meet at Clover Leaf restaurant. Let's say at seven?" "That's fine with me," responded Ted. He watched Adrianna as she headed back toward her station. *Ted this is the point of no return.'* The thought made him warm inside.

***

Clover Leaf restaurant was a three-star eating establishment. It catered to upscale clientele. The dress code there was formal attire. Adrianna was dressed in a ravishingly, tight-fitted, maroon colored dress. It was made from a light, airy, chiffon fabric. Tiny pearl earrings hung from her earlobes. Adrianna's makeup was sparsely applied. Her distinctive facial bone structure needed no masking. Her beauty radiated immensely. Adrianna's colorful, downward-turned eye sockets, narrow nose, and sensual lips displayed an erotic appearance. Her hair was done in a French braid twist. The sweet scent of jasmine emitted from her body.

Ted wore an immaculate, black, designer suit. He adorned a white shirt and black tie. Besides a watch, he wore no other jewelry.

"You clean up rather nicely," commented Adrianna. They were seated at a table for two.

"You are remarkably beautiful. Why hasn't anyone taken your lovely hand in marriage yet?"

Adrianna took a sip of champagne before answering the question. "I guess when I finished school my mind was just on my career. When I found my career, it seemed all the callers grew impatient and tired of waiting. It's the story of my life. Never having two needed things at the same time. I could have peanut butter but no jelly. Bread but no butter. Shoes but no socks. I could go on and on. How about you?"

Ted explained to her an edited version of his life. "At one time I was into religious studies, then I decided that I wanted to work in the medicine field. In one aspect I went from curing souls to healing bodies. I find both experiences gratifying."

"That's amazing but what about your love life?"

Ted stared into her bluish-green eyes. *I really like her and I don't want to lose her by lying to her.'* He sighed. "I'm going to be honest with you. Please don't make fun of what I'm about to say." He reached for his glass of champagne. He gulped the entire content before explaining. "To tell you the truth I am not experienced with the opposite sex." He watched her express change.

"You're not trying to tell me you're gay are you? I mean if you are that's your preference. At least you're being honest."

Ted held up a hand in protest. "No, no! I'm not gay. I grew up in the church. It was very strict about things of that nature. My family was very religious. I've never had a relationship with a woman." His eyes dropped toward his glass. It took Adrianna a moment to process the information. A thought caused her to chuckled. "You said that you wouldn't laugh."

"I'm not laughing, I am intrigued. You mean to tell me that you're a virgin? Why that's remarkable in this day and age. You are like a star, a historical figure or something. I'm impressed. I know it took courage for you to confide in me with your story. I'm honored."

The food arrived. They ate, conversed, and laughed. The evening was splendid. Ted liked Adrianna tremendously. Adrianna seemed to enjoy herself in Ted's company.

As the evening came to an end, a taxicab stopped in front of Adrianna's apartment building. It was a three-family brownstone structure located on a clean and secluded block in Brooklyn.

"I guess we're here. I want you to know I had a wonderful time."

"It doesn't have to end you know. Why don't you come up for a night cap?"

"I-I don't…"

"Sure you do. Come on silly." Adrianna pulled him by his tie toward the exit. As they were about to exit the vehicle, their attention was adverted by the taxi driver.

"The fare! That's 12 dollars and 75 cents." He was a small man of middle eastern descent. He wore designer frame eyewear. His head was turned toward the partition behind him.

Ted gazed at him through the plexiglass partition. "Excuse me…" Ted placed a 20 dollar bill through the glass. "Keep the change."

"Thank you."

Adrianna led him by his hand up the stone steps toward the front door. Ted noticed that Adrianna was intoxicated. He didn't want to take advantage of her.

"Are you sure this is a good idea?" He watched her fumble for the keys.

"Don't be silly of course I'm sure." She placed the key into the lock cylinder and turned. They entered a dim lit foyer that led to a staircase. Walnut finished steps creak as they trudged upon it. They stopped on the second floor landing. Adrianna inserted her key into the cylinder. A distinctive click sound reverberated in the quiet hall. She led him into a darken room. She began to fumble for the light switch. Halogen lamps illuminated the room. The living room came into view. A nicely decorated design of earth colors, plants, and paintings were a part of the decor. An elegant, brown sofa set gave the room a cozy ambiance. A natural parquet floor was immaculate.

"Have a seat. Would you like something to drink?" Adrianna began taking off her shoes.

"Yes, I'll have whatever you're having."

"Good! Then make us two gin tonics on the rocks. The bar is over there…" She pointed to the opposite side of the room. "I'll just be a moment. I have to get out of this dress." Adrianna disappeared into another room.

Ted busied himself at the mini bar. It was located in the corner of the room. The bar held a small electric ice box, two wooden stools, and a mirror designed wall. The mirrors gave the illusion of more bottles. Ted finished making the drinks and carried them to a glass table near the sofa. The distinctive sound of ice clinging against the glasses resonated as he placed them on coasters.

Adrianna exited the bedroom wearing comfortable lounge wear. The outfit held a heart shaped emblem with monogram initials VS. It was located in the center of the panty line. Ted knew the initials belonged to the famous designer Victoria Secrets. The loose fitting ensemble were just cotton pajama pants with lace trimming. The top was a belly shirt made from the same material. Adrianna's flat stomach revealed a pierced navel ring. Her creamy skin and curved hips excited Ted. She let her hair flow down her back. The sandy color of her hair matched the decor of the room. Adrianna approached the couch and sat next to Ted. He picked up the drinks and handed one to her.

"Let's toast," requested Adrianna.

"Okay, in reference to what?

"Us, as in a new beginning."

"Okay, I really like that." The two glasses touched. A fine high-pitched sound reverberated in the room.

Adrianna gulped down half of the content in the glass. She walked over to the entertainment center and touched a button. Enormous, rich sound filled the room. The genre of music was smooth contemporary jazz. The sound was omnipresent; the surround sound was amazing. The clarity was distinctive.

Adrianna sat close to Ted. "Relax, let me help you." She helped him out of his jacket and tie. She began to loosen his top shirt button. "That's more like it."

The two gazed into one another's eyes. "Let me ease your curiosity. All you have to do is relax and I'll make it happen." Adrianna took Ted by the hand. She led him into the bedroom.

The bedroom was just as elegant as the living room. Lavender and cream was the main color scheme. The bedding matched the painted walls perfectly. Ted noticed the mirrored ceiling over the bed. His thoughts caused him to smile. Deep inside he was nervous. Adrianna sat next to him on the edge of the bed.

"Relax."

"Are you sure this is a good idea?"

Adrianna giggled. She found him charming. He reminded her of a school kid. The effects from the alcohol was overbearing upon her. "Yes, I think it's a perfect idea. How long do you plan on holding onto your cherry?" Giggles added to her merriment. She pushed Ted back onto the bed. "Now, relax and let me show you how it's done."

Ted was beyond nervousness. His body was tense. The unsureness of his ability to perform overwhelmed him. Surprisingly, Adrianna's touch caused him arousal. He allowed Adrianna to undress him. After the tie, the shirt came off. Within minutes Ted was stark naked on the bed. He was adorned in nothing but his black dress socks.

Adrianna stood aback from the bed. She was in plain view of Ted. Slowly, she began to undress in a burlesque manner. First, she removed her belly shirt. The exposure of her perfect breasts were visible. They were symmetrically perfect with pink aureoles and erect nipples on firm breast. Her breast remained upright even after the bra was removed. With the sound of smooth jazz in the background, Adrianna began gyrating to the music. She gently squeezed her breasts together. Ted noticed her seduction had a profound effect on him. She continued to remove her pants. Her curvaceous figure and creamy skin was now visible. She allowed her sandy color hair to hang down her back.

Adrianna slowly approached the bed. Gently, she straddled Ted.

Looking down from above, she allowed her breasts to touch his lips. Ted reached for them feeling the softness of her skin. Hungrily, he moistened his lip and licked around her aureoles and nipples.

Adrianna moaned in pure pleasure. She pulled away kissing his neck while slowly making her way down his chest. Her tongue flickered on his nipples. Ted gave off a soft moan. What he was experiencing was completely new. Adrianna continued down his body and stopping at his swollen member.

Placing his shaft into her warm moistened mouth, she began sucking while keeping her left hand firmly grasped around his love muscle. She jerked his member up and down, keeping her soft fleshy lips and wet tongue upon his penis. Adrianna eyed Ted to see his eyes were closed.

"Come, get inside of me." She lie on her back with her legs gaped. The position gave Ted a clear view into her most private world.

Ted gazed at her furry pink mound. Her sandy colored hair turned him on. He knew what to do. It's just he'd never done it before. *Well here goes...'*

"Just be gentle with me."

Ted entered into her dark moist abyss. Adrianna's vaginal muscles tingled. The sensation was indescribable. He opened his eyes to see that Adrianna was in a fervent way. Her hips gyrated toward his thrust. He could feel her vaginal muscles pulsate against his hard shaft. As the tempo heightened, so did their breathing. Suddenly, a sensation he'd never experienced commanded his body. Ted felt that he was no longer in control. For a moment his mind was fixated on his clerical teachings. He thought he was being possessed by a presence. The sensation was surreal. His body began to shudder. He couldn't control his thrusting motion into Adrianna's orifice. His penis throbbed as he ejaculated. The two were left drained and exhausted. Adrianna was panting for air. Her hair was disheveled.

"That was something huh?"

"You bet!" Ted watched as Adrianna quickly raced from the bed holding her crotch. She was trying to keep the semen from seeping out onto the bed or floor.

Adrianna returned with a basin filled with warm, soapy water. She began washing his genitals with a washcloth. The water relaxed him. For a moment he felt like an infant being changed.

"I'm going to take a bath. If you want there's a shower stall in the bathroom. Unless you want to take a bath with me." Adrianna smiled as she sauntered toward the bathroom.

Ted couldn't believe how good he felt. Suddenly, he felt revived. He felt recharged. Ted stood and headed into the bathroom.

9

A black sedan with dark tinted windows came to a stop one half a block away from All Saints Church. A disoriented figure was discharged. The figure wore an eyeless ski mask on her head; it was used to confuse her as to her whereabouts.

Afraid to move, she stood still after being released. She was too afraid to remove the headwear placed upon her. It wasn't until she heard the vehicle drive off into the far distance that she noticed that the block was quiet. Time held no significance to her. She snatched the mask from her head. Slowly, her eyes adjusted to the intensity of light associated with the nocturnal setting. The street lights cast a hazy iridescence of neon colors. Her equilibrium was slightly impaired. It was due to the effects of the drugs that was administered to her.

Sister Beatrice began to shiver as she thought about the abduction. She couldn't remember any of it. She had not witness any faces. She had spent the entire ordeal unconscious, she was oblivious to any of the acts that preceded. Tears fell from her face. Her legs gave out from under her because of the hours of not using her muscles. She dropped to the pavement. The thoughts of being raped by a diseased psychopath overwhelmed her.

A stranger approached. He wore a denim jacket with matching pants. Being a local to the area, he was familiar with the nuns. He continually donated to all of the fund raisers the church offered. It was the same church that he attended from time to time. His black hair was neatly tucked under a baseball cap of his favorite team. Small beady eyes and thick eyebrows gave him a distinctive appearance. He saw that the nun looked disoriented and her habit was wrinkled and soiled.

"Sister are you all right? What happened? Are you hurt?" He held out a hand to help her to stand.

Sister Beatrice felt uneasy. Her head was spinning with different thoughts. At first glimpse, she thought the man standing in front of her was the abductor. She had no way of knowing.

"Sister, let me help you up."

Sister Beatrice allowed the stranger to help her to stand upright. "Thank you."

"Where would you like to go? Back to the church?" Sister Beatrice nodded. She couldn't answer because her throat was parched, another side effect from the drugs. Stabilizing her hand with his, they headed toward the church.

As they entered the structure, a nun dressed in a black habit rushed toward them when she saw Sister Beatrice. For days everyone was worried about her wellbeing.

"Oh my!" She placed a hand to her mouth. "Where have you been? We've been so worried about you. I've prayed so hard for your safe return. God is good." The nun noticed the stranger.

"I'm Andrew Meyers. I found her down the street. She looked shaken and distraught. I brought her here."

"Thank you. My name is sister Ramirez. Again, thank you for your kind service. I'll take it from here."

"Okay sister." Andrew Meyers exited the building.

Sister Ramirez attention was adverted to Sister Beatrice. "Good heaven child! What happen to you?" She saw at that moment that Sister Beatrice looked disarrayed. Her hair was disheveled. Sister Beatrice didn't answer. She held a far away gaze in her eyes. She stared as if she was looking into another time. She gazed around at the familiar setting. "Never mind! Let's get you to your room. Priest Hamilton is in a prayer service right now. He should be done shortly. He'll know what to do."

***

After washing and changing clothing, Sister Beatrice lie in bed staring up at the ceiling. Although she was tired, sleep evaded her. Cacophonous noise entered her mind. Her mind produced a cornucopia of thoughts. She closed her eyes tightly and placed her hands over her ears in an attempt to dispel the sounds. The effort was useless. Suddenly, a knock came to the door. The sound jolted her from her reverie.

"You may enter." The tone of her voice was drained of emotions.

Priest Hamilton entered. He was dressed in a long, black frock. The garment had purple trimming down the center and around the edges. It was a ceremonial habit used for prayer service. He approached the bed and took Sister Beatrice by the hand. "Our prayers have been answered child. Did they hurt you?" Sister Beatrice didn't answer. Priest Hamilton sat in a chair adjacent to the bed. "The good thing is you're safe."

Sister Beatrice looked toward Carl. Seeing the familiar face caused the ducts in the corner of her eyes to collapse. Uncontrollable tears flowed down her cheeks as she sat up to face the priest. She began recalling the moments of the ordeal.

"They placed a chemically treated cloth over my nose and mouth. I was forcefully placed into a van…" She hesitated for a moment, the recollection of thoughts was disheartening. She tried to regain her composure. "That is all that I can remember. I have no recollection of how long I've been gone."

"Three days."

"Why would anyone do that to me? I've never harmed a soul."

Carl patted her on the shoulder. "Of course you haven't. Everybody has been concerned. The police have been investigating your disappearance." He stood. "In fact, I'll call them now." Carl Hamilton left the room.

***

Detective Hall placed the receiver on the cradle. The call was quite unusual. He stood and placed his jacket on. He grabbed his keys from the desk and headed out the door.

He exited the unmarked sedan and headed toward the church. Anxious to know the details, he rushed inside. He saw Priest Hamilton speaking with a nun. He approached.

"Where is she?" The priest pointed to a door. The detective knocked sternly. He heard a voice on the other side of the door. He entered to see Sister Beatrice standing and looking out of the window. She turned as Detective Hall entered.

"Hi, my name is Detective Hall. I am assigned to your case. May I tell you something? You are much adored around these parts. Is there anything you can remember about the captor?"

Sister Beatrice studied the man in front of her. Besides having a wonderful complexion, she noticed his smile. The way his pearly white teeth radiated in his mouth. "All I can remember is exiting the stationary store with supplies for my class. As I crossed Main Street, a black, cargo van pulled in front of me. It blocked my path."

"Did you get a glimpse of the men inside of the van? I want you to take your time and concentrate."

"No! Two men wearing masks jumped out and placed a material over my nose and mouth. Afterward, everything went blank. I don't know how long I've been captive or if I've been raped."

"Okay, I understand. The first thing we're going to have to do is get you to the hospital. If there is DNA involved, we'll get the perpetrators." Detective Hall began to take the case personally.

10

An unmarked gray sedan stopped in front of Westchester General Hospital. Detective Hall and Sister Beatrice exited the vehicle. A barrage of media personnel and camera crews besieged them. Lights, cameras, and flash bulbs illuminated the scene.

Sister Beatrice suddenly became fearful. Detective Hall sensed her apprehension. He grasped her by the forearm and led her toward the building. *'How did the news get out?'*

"Sister Beatrice, were you able to identify your abductor's?" asked a local news correspondent.

Detective Hall whispered to Sister Beatrice. "Don't answer, just continue walking."

Another news spokesperson thrusted a microphone in front of her face. "In the three days of your abduction were you sexually abused?"

"Was ransom paid for your release by the church?"

"Detective Hall, is this case settled as far as the police department is concerned? Now that Sister Beatrice is back with us?"

Sister Beatrice and Detective Hall continued through the hospital's entrance door. The mass media frenzy was left behind. It was one of the places the media weren't allowed without a permit. The commotion that it caused would disrupted the flow of the hospital.

A nurse met them in the lobby with a wheelchair. The nurse was a short stature, middle-aged woman. She was very attractive. Her name tag read J. Higgins.

"Please have a seat. I will take you to the emergency room. The doctor is awaiting your arrival."

Exiting the elevator on the third floor, they turned right and headed down a long corridor. A seating area came into view. Plastic seats were placed in the middle of the section. Treated wood benches were placed along the perimeter. Detective Hall noticed a few vending machines in the corner.

The nurse stopped. "I'm sorry detective, you'll have to wait here while Sister Beatrice is being examined."

"Sure."

Sister Beatrice was wheeled into a room that held stainless-steel countertops and tables. Different monitors were lined along a wall. A woman in a white, laboratory coat stood with an outstretched hand. Her hair was black and lengthy.

"Hi, my name is Doctor Sutherland. Please, have a seat on the table."

Sister Beatrice instantly took notice of the doctor's dark complexion. It was the way the doctor's skin tone radiated that amazed her. She also notice the doctor's curvaceous body underneath. *'She's young and vibrant.'* Suddenly, she felt tensed.

"Relax, I'm just going to give you a thorough examination." Dr Sutherland took an ophthalmoscope and began examine Sister Beatrice's eyes. The doctor noticed her pupils were dilated. "Are you feeling sluggish or morose at the moment?"

Sister Beatrice nodded. "Slightly, but more so earlier."

"Please, stick out your tongue." The doctor placed a wooden tongue suppressor in her mouth to examine her tonsils. "Okay, I'm now going to do a blood workup on you to find out what kind of chemicals they used to cause your unconscious state." The procedure lasted only a few minutes. "Sister Beatrice I need for you to go behind that partition and put on this gown." Dr Sutherland handed her a sky blue garment. As Sister Beatrice went to change, Dr Sutherland began jotting notes onto a form. Sister Beatrice returned.

"Please, lie face up on the table and place your legs in the stirrups." Afterward, she began to examine Sister Beatrice's vaginal opening. She took DNA swab samples. The doctor also notice her hymen was still intact. "You're still a virgin thank goodness." After securing the samples, she removed the latex gloves she wore. "That will be all. Tomorrow I will notify you of the results. You may change."

"Thank you doctor."

11

News reporters from major networks jockeyed for position in front of All Saints Church. Priest Carl Hamilton was at a podium located near the entrance. A dozen microphones were stationed on the podium.

"Yes, I truly believe that God is at work here. This church has come through its share of struggles to become a true worship place of God. I think that Sister Beatrice's abduction was a test to the faith of the church. Our prayers were heard and answered. It is the only explanation to this bizarre situation. There are no clues, no leads. Something that is highly unusual in a case as such. That is because when God acts, man cannot intervene. Today was a confirmation that God is with this church. Using a good hearted vessel as Sister

Beatrice, God has displayed his mercy and power for us to witness."

The crowd outside the church began to grow. People and vehicles stopped to see what was taking place in their quiet little town of Yonkers, New York.

"So you're saying all of this was a miraculous act of God?" asked a reporter. He stood on the top step near the podium.

"Yes." A camera flash illuminated in the priest's face. "I believe that this church is in direct lineage to God."

The crowd outside the church began to grow more intensely. Flashes began flickering quickly and successively by the media. Murmuring from the crowd ensued. Another reporter shouted a question to Priest Hamilton.

"You talk as if this wasn't a criminal act. Are you saying that the charges for Sister Beatrice's abductors will be dropped?"

"What I am saying..." All eyes turned toward a gray unmarked sedan approaching through the crowd. A parting of the crowd allowed the vehicle to pass. The vehicle headed toward the church. Emergency lights flashed atop the vehicle.

As Detective Hall steered the official vehicle onto the block of the church, he and Sister Beatrice noticed the large assembly in front of the church.

"I wonder what is going on?" asked Sister Beatrice. Her mind thought the worst.

As they neared, Detective Hall saw the media. He also witnessed Priest Hamilton at the podium. "I hope he isn't speaking about the case with the media."

As they exited the vehicle they were accosted by the story-hungered frenzy of the media. In a matter of seconds, all of the attention of the crowd was diverted from Priest Hamilton to Detective Hall and Sister Beatrice as they exited the vehicle. Microphones were thrust toward their faces. A barrage of explosive questions were being asked simultaneously. The harsh noise was deafening to Sister Beatrice. She placed her hands to her ears. Ignoring the inquiries, they continued toward the entrance. They came into contact with Priest Hamilton.

"I am glad you are back. These people are concerned about you," said the priest to Sister Beatrice.

Detective Hall gazed at all the spectators. He knew the perpetrators could be in the crowd. His attention went to the priest. "Priest Hamilton, what is this all about? I hope you didn't say anything that could taint this investigation." The detective became irate seeing the massive crowd gathered.

"I've only spoken the truth, that's all I know."

"Okay, let's get inside." Detective Hall escorted them into the building.

The sanctuary of the church buffered the commotion that hovered outside. Sister Beatrice was disturbed by the fiasco. Everything was happening too fast for her to conceive the ramifications of the ordeal.

"May I please be excused?" She referred to the priest.

"Yes my child. Please, rest yourself. I know it's been a tiring day for you," responded the priest. His attention was adverted to the detective. "I want to thank you for everything you've done in this matter. As you know, I do not feel this is a police matter."

"You what?" Detective Hall's voice became stern. "Then what do you believe this is?"

"I believe it was a divine intervention."

Detective Hall was dumbfounded at the answer. "Priest, I'm not trying to blaspheme but an abduction is a criminal act. Maybe getting her back safely is a divine act but a crime was committed."

"Sir, an argument I will not assist in. I can only tell you what God tells me." He kissed the silver cross that he wore on a long chain around his neck. "Now, if you will excuse me I'm expected at a service." Priest Hamilton walked away leaving Detective Hall to stare at his back. The detective was baffled.

'I might have to find a way to check into this.' The priest's demeanor troubled him. Detective Hall couldn't quite place a finger on it.

FOUR

WEEKS

LATER

12

Adrianna Houghton spent the weekend alone at home. Today she'd awakened not feeling well. A nauseating feeling, mixed with an upset stomach overwhelmed her. She couldn't figure it out because she'd never been sick. The most she'd ever suffered from was a common cold.

Trying to clear her mind, she turned on the television to her favorite game show. Adrianna found joy in answering the questions before the contestants had a chance to answer.

She thought about Ted Conwell. *'He's fun to be around. Now that I've opened Pandora's Box what have I created? He's sexually insatiable.'* Her thoughts brought about a smile.

Suddenly, a wrenching pain enveloped inside her stomach. The excruciating pain caused her to hold her hands to the area that caused her discomfort. Without warning, a bubbling sensation began to form within. Bile ascended from her depth toward her throat. She stood from her seated position on the couch and rushed toward the bathroom.

Adrianna bent over the stool and began to vomit into the commode. Her discharge was dry heaves. A strong barfing noise ensued from deep inside. The display of spasmodic attacks were involuntary. *'What is wrong with me?'* After the attacks subsided, she washed her face and brushed her teeth. Adrianna stood in front of the mirror staring at her reflection. She noticed her sandy colored hair was disheveled.

Inside the bedroom, she picked up the telephone and called the company's doctor for a checkup.

***

After the examination, Adrianna sat in a waiting area for the test results. She used the downtime to check her messages on the social networks. It was one of her favorite pastimes.

One hour later, a woman wearing a three-quarter length, white, laboratory coat entered the waiting area from a side door. She was a middle-aged woman. Her hair was black and lengthy. Her creamy skin and blue eyes were bright as pastels in the fluorescent lighting.

"Miss Houghton, please follow me." They headed through a door.

A long carpeted corridor came into view. They traveled down the lengthy hall. Oakwood doors were on both sides of the corridor. They stopped at door number five. Inside, an examination room came into view. State-of-the-art equipment lined the room.

"Please, Miss Houghton take a seat," requested the doctor. She wore a name tag that read P Palmer.

Adrianna sat opposite from the doctor who sat behind her desk. She studied the doctor's eyes and demeanor trying to get a predisposition of the results. The doctor's facial expression gave nothing away.

"I have the results. You are pregnant." The doctor's eyes moved from the document to meet Adrianna's eyes. She noticed the surprise expression on her face. "My concern is in your white blood cells. The deteriorating condition causes me concern. I went back and double check."

"I don't understand any of what you are saying." Anxiety penetrated her being.

"You are diagnosed as HIV positive."

Adrianna stood abruptly. "That can't be right! I-I don't know anyone who has AIDS…" Adrianna hesitated as her mind recollected her movements. *'Ted Conwell…'* Anger permeated her being along with fear.

"The results are accurate. You're still in the early stages to abort the pregnancy if you decide to do so. 85 percent chances is that your baby will contract the virus."

Adrianna sat with her face buried in her hands. Frustration began to cloud her judgement. *'How could this be happening to me?'*

"Miss Houghton we have an excellent counseling staff aboard.

Would you like to be scheduled?"

"No! That will not be necessary. As far as the abortion is concerned yes, I would like an abortion." She wiped the tears from her eyes. Her mascara was smeared in the process. A strange sensation emitted from deep within. It was anger mixed with hatred.

13

Ted Conwell couldn't believe how vibrant life really was. Adrianna had sparked a force that was once dormant inside of him. Now that it was awakened, he felt as if he could take on the world. Being with Adrianna brought him pure delight. He enjoyed the times they spent away from the work environment. It was as if they were roll-playing two different characters. One at work, and the other in their personal space. The thought caused him to smile. He looked over at her station to find it unoccupied another day. Adriana hadn't returned any of his calls. *'Something is wrong, I can feel it.'* Ted decided to go home early today.

Ted Conwell fixed himself an alcoholic beverage. He kicked off his shoes and sat on the couch. The living room was his favorite space for relaxation. He replayed his last encounter with Adrianna to see what went wrong. His cellphone rang. Rushing to the kitchen table, he picked up the device on the third ring.

"Hello? Adrianna?" He listened the the caller.

"No, it's me Carl. I just wanted to thank you and to let you know that when the money start piling in you will get your cut."

"Money? Is that what that was all about? Did you see the news coverage? I think you're going to bring in more attention to yourself than you'll know what to do with."

Carl chuckled. "You worry too much. Let me do the thinking."

"No! In fact, I don't want anything to do with this scheme of yours. I came here to find a new start."

"And a new start you shall have. Don't you want to spoil Adrianna?" There was a silence on the line by Ted. The sound of Adrianna's name coming from Carl's mouth sounded cynical.

"Ted? Are you still there?"

"Yes, I'm here. Do not go near her…"

"Or what?" Carl angrily waited for a reply. None came afterward.

Just as I thought.' He was satisfied with the effect of the moment. "As I was saying, when this is over we'll take a plane out of the country."

Ted realized at that moment he was dealing with a crazed man. Over the years something snapped inside of Carl. Ted had no intentions of letting Adrianna get hurt. "What do you want from me?"

"Nothing, just keep yourself available." The line was disconnected.

Ted Conwell stared at the receiver as if it were a foreign object. *'Something has to be done about Carl.'* After the call, Ted became a nervous wreck. He felt uneasy about the entire situation. After a few more drinks, Ted was fast asleep on the sofa.

14

Adrianna exited the abortion clinic feeling empty inside. The pain in her stomach was a reminder of what had taken place. She wore dark sunglasses to hide her true feelings. She didn't want the world to know that she'd messed up big time.

Adrianna went from having everything to having nothing. She felt as if she made a deal with the devil by trading all of her wealth for a deadly virus. A virus that now resided inside. It continued grew as time passed. Adrianna realized she was a host to a parasite that would eventually kill her. She flagged a taxicab and instructed the driver to take her to a restaurant located on the corner from her residence.

Inside the cafe, she noticed the pleasant ambiance. She glanced at customers sitting at tables. Some seemed to be enjoying one another's company. Others were using the store's wifi to connect with the internet. She saw people using laptop computers to write as they enjoyed the delicious beverages. A distinctive aroma of fresh coffees lingered in the air leaving delightful scents.

Adrianna found a seat at a booth. She ordered two lattes coffees. She was in the smoking section; it was something that she'd never indulged in. Today was different. *There will be plenty of things I'll do that I've never done before.'* She opening the package of cigarets and extracted one. After lighting the cigarette, she deeply inhaled the pungent smoke. She exhaled a grayish-blue cloud of fumes. Adrianna wanted to gag but fought hard to control the urge. She sat looking out of the window as traffic and pedestrians passed. Everyone seemed oblivious that she existed. *'I can not go on like this. No I won't!'* Images of Ted Conwell entered into her mental space. Anger permeated her emotions. She thought about the conversation she would have with him. *'I asked you and you said you weren't gay. But you gave me a terrible disease. All I was trying to do was free you from your ignorance of pleasure. Now look what you've done to me…'* Adrianna stood. Frustrated, she walked away from the table, leaving the entire pack of cigarettes and two empty cups. She exited the cafe and headed for home.

Adrianna spent the afternoon on the floor of her living room. She stared toward the bedroom. She was afraid to enter the space. Her depressed state of mind magnified greatly. After downing half of the contents from a bottle of scotch, she stared blankly into the bedroom. Her focus was mainly on the bed. She pictured it being more than a sleeping apparatus. In Adrianna's cognizance, it was now an instrument of death. *'I'll never sleep there again.'*

After a while Adrianna found herself walking the streets with her handbag clutched tightly to her side. She walked into a Chase bank and withdrew her entire savings account. She also removed other securities. She took her belongings to a table in the bank and placed the contents into a yellow envelope. She address the heft package to her mother. She wrote a short letter and sealed the package. Using her cellphone, Adrianna placed a call to Ted. She explained to him that she needed to meet him at his home.

***

Dress in a black, denim pants suit, Adrianna clutched her designer tote bag close to her body. After knocking on the door, she stood back allowing herself to be view through the peephole. She could hear the security chain rattling as it was being removed.

The door was opened by Ted Conwell. He was wearing shorts and and a white tee shirt. Leather slippers adorned his feet.

"Adrianna! I've been so worried about you. Come in…" He stepped aside to allow her access. Adrianna stepped through the threshold. "Have a seat. Can I get you something to drink or eat?" Ted ran his hand through his hair briskly. The visit was unexpected. The apartment was disorganized. There were magazines on the floor and leftover food on the table.

The untidiness of the place didn't seem to bother Adrianna. She accepted the offer. "I'll have a scotch with no water or ice."

Ted studied her for a moment after she ordered. *That tough huh?*' He walked toward the makeshift bar in the corner of the room. With his back turned toward Adrianna, he began pouring the drinks.

Adrianna used the time to reached into her tote bag. The item in question brought her comfort. She reached in and retrieved a pack of cigarettes. Ted returned with the drinks. He handed one to Adrianna and sat beside her.

"Do you mind if I smoke?" she asked.

"I didn't know that you smoked. Sure, go right ahead." At that moment, Ted felt an unsettling sensation brewing. He wasn't able to pinpoint the root of its origin.

"There's a lot of things we'll have to find out about one another I guess. Some the hard way." Adrianna lit the cigarette and took in a deep inhalation of the fumes. She expelled a grayish-blue cloud into the atmosphere.

"Where have you been? You haven't been at work. You haven't returned any of my calls. What's going on?"

Adrianna didn't respond right away. She finished her drink. She took another toke on the cigarette. Adrianna placed both items on the coffee table as she kept her eyes locked with Ted's. "I've been busy. In fact, I've been betrayed, deceived, and lied to." The sound of her voice changed. Harsh anger resonated in her tone.

"Adrianna I don't know what you're talking about."

"I'll tell you…" Adrianna sighed deeply. "I awoke yesterday feeling ill. I went to the doctor to find out that I was pregnant."

Ted was taken aback by the statement. "Why I-I think that's great!"

Ted became excited because he really like Adrianna. He knew that if given the chance, he'd do anything to make it work with her. "Don't worry I'll take care…"

"Listen!" She interjected. She drew her tote bag near, placing her left hand inside. "That's not all. I've been also diagnosed as having HIV viral."

"What are you saying?" Ted became alarmed. "I don't know how that could be unless you…" He couldn't finish the sentence. The thought was painful.

"Don't you sit there and try to soften things up. You're the only person I've had relations with. Prior to that, it had been six months. You stared me in the face when I asked you about being gay…"

"I'm not a homosexual?"

"Then how could this have happened?"

Ted stood. "Adrianna please…" A frightful expression was displayed on his face as he stared at Adrianna's left hand.

Adrianna removed her hand from her tote bag. As she did, a black, .380 caliber, semi-automatic, handgun became visible. She pointed the menacing weapon at Ted. "Sit down! I'm not finished." Her tone became cynical. She spoke low with control. "I'll ask you again. If you were a virgin as you claimed, how could you have contracted the virus?"

Ted Conwell fearfully stared at the weapon. He'd never been placed in such a perilous situation. "The only encounters that I have been in sexually was by force. It was done through molestation when I was a boy." Ted went on to explain the entire accounts of his life in the church. Emotionally charged, he held his face in his hands. "I was constantly abused by the bishop of the church where I attended."

"Where is he now?"

"Dead."

"Why didn't you tell me before I made love to you? You didn't give me a chance to decide properly."

"I had no idea. I have no symptoms of any disease. How was I to know?" He looked from the weapon to Adrianna's bluish-green eyes. She seemed to have aged since he'd saw her last. "Now what?"

"Now what? My life is over before it ever began thanks to you." Tears streamed down her cheeks. "I had an abortion today. Do you have any idea what that feels like?" Ted didn't respond. "It feels as if your insides are being ripped out. It leaves you feeling hollow, violated, and void."

"Adrianna I'm sorry. Please put down the gun. Let's talk about it. There's got to be a solution to this." His body began to tremble at the thought of death.

Unmoved emotionally by his explanation, Adrianna kept the weapon trained on Ted. "This is the solution…" She gestured with the weapon by waving it. "We are no longer able to share what we had once been placed here to share. Whoever we touch from this moment on will become affected with this vile disease." She stared at him disdainfully. "No! That can't be allowed to happen."

"But I need…"

PLOP!

A thunderous blast emitted from the barrel of the small caliber handgun. The sound was loud. A deafening noise that left a ringing sensation in Adrianna's ears. Malodorous stench of heated cordite permeated the air. The ejected projectile's trajectory was aimed at Ted's chest. The point of contact was just above the solar plexus region. His once white shirt became saturated with a crimson hue. His eyes opened wide upon impact. Feeling disenchanted, he couldn't believe he'd been shot.

Excruciating pain enveloped his chest. Two of is ribs were shattered from the fragments of the projectile. Ted gazed at his wound. He refocused his stare toward Adrianna. He was in total disbelief. "Y-You shot me!"

Adrianna stood as the sofa became saturated with his blood. "You must die Ted."

PLOP!

Another thunderous clap emitted from the weapon. This time, Ted lie slumped and unmoving on the sofa. His eyes were closed. The projectile entered his body at his right temple. Blood trickled onto his face.

The sounds of sirens in the far distance crescendoed in the small room. Adrianna figured that someone in the building must have heard the blast sounds and notified the authorities. Adrianna approached the window and stared outside. She could see the flashing lights nearing in the distance.

Adrianna made a decision. She walked over to the bar and picked up a bottle of scotch off of the counter. The amber colored liquid glistened from the room lighting. Picking up her cigarette pack, she removed one. She placed the cigarette to her mouth and lit it. The weapon was positioned in her right hand. The liquor bottle and the cigarette in the other. She headed back toward the window. Blue and red flashing lights danced atop police vehicles. The scene displayed urgency. Adrianna saw uniformed officers rushing into the building with weapons drawn.

Quickly, she tilted her head back with the scotch bottle in her mouth. The golden colored liquid produced air bubbles as she gulped down the spirit. A burning sensations erupted in her stomach. She took a deep inhalation of smoke from the cigarette. Hard, rapid knocks came to the door.

"Police! Open the door!" The demand was said forcefully.

Adrianna gazed at Ted's body for a moment. Without hesitation, she placed the barrel of the weapon in her mouth. She squeezed the trigger. The bullet exited out the back of her skull as she dropped to the floor. Fragments of bone, blood, and gore splattered on the wall behind her.

At that instant, the front door burst into pieces and splinters from forced entry. Officers rushed into the apartment with their weapons drawn. After securing the apartment, the authorities tended to the crime scene. Crowds of spectators amounted in the front of the building. The officers were careful not to disturb anything in the apartment. The officer in charge radioed dispatch and notified them of the situation.

15

Detective Hall and Sister Beatrice sat in Dr Sutherland's office listening to the results of the test that Sister Beatrice had underwent yesterday.

"As far as I could see the reports indicate you are in good physical condition, and you were never sexually penetrated. You are still a virgin. There was no foreign matter found to suggest any additional DNA sampling. I'd have to say you were lucky or blessed.

"I'd prefer to use the word blessed," said Sister Beatrice. She felt relieved after hearing the results.

Detective Hall sighed deeply. He had anticipated finding a relative clue. Disappointment was displayed on his face. He stood and shook hands with Dr Sutherland.

"Thank you for your time and expert opinion doctor."

"My pleasure, if there's anything else I can do to help you in this matter you can count on me."

A smile was displayed on Sister Beatrice's face.

***

Detective Hall stopped the unmarked sedan in front of All Saint Church. Sister Beatrice exited on the passenger side. An announcement came on the two-way radio in the vehicle. It was the dispatcher calling a numbered code for Detective Hall.

"I'm sorry Sister Beatrice, this call is for me. I have to take it. I will call you when something becomes available. In fact, take this..." He handed her a business card. "Call me anytime."

Sister Beatrice received the card. She closed the vehicle's door and stepped onto the sidewalk. The gray sedan raced down the road with its lights illuminated and the siren blaring. Feeling enlightened because of the news from the doctor, Sister Beatrice headed inside the church.

***

Detective Hall approached the crime scene on the residential block in Brooklyn. He witnessed a massive crowd along with police activity in the vicinity.

Exiting the vehicle, Detective Hall ducked under a yellow crime scene tape. It was used to cordoned off the area from the onlookers. News medias were on the scene, all hoping to get an exclusive story out on the airwaves. Detective Hall was met by a uniformed officer. They shook hands.

"My name is Lieutenant Cushman."

"Detective Hall lieutenant. What do you have?"

"It appears to be a murder suicide. It looks to be a domestic dispute between lovers that went bad."

They entered the building, finding their way into the apartment that was now a crime scene.

Detective Hall transformed all of his energy into the matter at hand. It was one of his outstanding traits that excelled his discovery skill over the rest. Detective Hall had an eye for detail. He placed on a pair of sky blue, latex gloves given to him by the lieutenant. He began methodically retracing the crime scene. The lieutenant followed along.

"It looks like the two sat on this couch talking for a while."

"How can you tell that?" asked the Lieutenant Cushman. He was perplexed at the suggestion.

"The cigarette in the ashtray has lipstick on it. It is also extinguished at the very end. If it had burned on its own the filter would have still been intact. Second, there's a trace of indentation on the sofa next to the body. He was shot twice but not from a moving position. There's no sign if a struggle or displacement around the room or around his body. It looks like he took the first hit from close range right here..." Detective Hall pointed to the seat next to the body. "The next slug looks to have been made from this angle. Afterward, the shooter stood near the window in an intoxicated state and blew her own brains out."

"Wow! That's amazing how you can analyze a situation."

"Lieutenant have you called in forensic yet?"

"Yes sir, they're on the way."

"Okay, make sure nothing in this apartment is disturbed. Make sure I get a copy of all evidence and photographs from the lab boys."

"Yes sir."

SIX

WEEKS

LATER

16

**ALL SAINT CHURCH
CHURCH RECTORY
2:32 AM**

Sister Beatrice was having a fitful sleep until sharp stabs of excruciating pain overtook her peaceful somnolency. The unfamiliar sensation had awaken her abruptly. She tried to stand but doubled over on the floor. The cold, hardwood floor caused her to awaken fully. She shivered from the floor temperature.

"Ooww!" Sister Beatrice screamed out in anguish. The room was dark. The only light in the area was emitted from the hallway. The illumination crept in from a separation under the door.

Suddenly, the sounds of bare feet pattered on the hardwood floor. The door rushed open. Two nightgown-clad nuns hurried into the room. The overhead light abruptly filled the room. They saw Sister Beatrice on the floor in distress. Instinctively, they sprang into action.

"Sister Beatrice! Oh my!" exclaimed Sister Lawrence. She helped Sister Beatrice back onto the bed. "What is it child? Where does it hurt?" Unable to answer, Sister Beatrice grimaced in agony.

Sister Winslet, another nun, rushed into the room. She took one look at the scene and rushed out to call for assistance. She returned a short time after with Priest Hamilton. The priest held a knowing expression. *'I had wondered if it would actually work.'* Moments after, the sound of sirens was audible from outside. The priest went to meet them. Sister Beatrice continued holding her stomach with both hands.

Two paramedics entered the room. Both were middle-aged men. One was tall and slim with a powdery, pale complexion and a slight oblong head. The other was medium build with a round face. His sandy brown hair and grayish-green eyes were distinctive. They saw that Sister Beatrice was in pain. Methodically, they sprang into action.

"How long has she been like this?" asked the tall medical technician. He was taking a pulse reading from her arm.

Sister Lawrence spoke. "I heard a noise about twenty minutes ago. I came in here to find Sister Beatrice on the floor. Sister Carmen and I placed her back onto the bed."

The technician with the sandy brown colored hair focused a light into Sister Beatrice's eyes. "Sister can you hear me?" Sister Beatrice remained unresponsive.

Together, the two medical technicians placed Sister Beatrice on a collapsible gurney. They whisked her away toward the ambulance. Sister Lawrence and Priest Hamilton traveled along in the rear compartment. Both silently prayed during the entire trip.

***

Carl was beginning to feel apprehensive about the entire ordeal. He'd done everything in his power to perfect a massive following. *'Having the media is an ingenious idea.'* For a while he thought the primal part of the plan was ineffective. When Sister Winslet rushed into the room in the middle of the night, he knew exactly what was taking place.

The ambulance stopped at King's County hospital. Sister Beatrice was rushed into the emergency room. Priest Hamilton and Sister Lawrence were made to wait in a designated area. The room held uncomfortable plastic seats that linked together. A few vending machines were placed in a corner. The public address system blared overhead. The sound of staff being paged was broadcast constantly. In the early hours of the morning, the area was congested with parents and relatives waiting. It was a silent presence to the old adage, *'New Yorkers never sleep.'*

Sister Lawrence sat in a seat with her eyes closed. She was fingering rosary beads that were worn around her neck. Priest Hamilton paced inside the small confined space. A discarded newspaper attracted his attention. Picking up the newspaper from the floor, he sat and read the cover article. He was completely taken by surprise as he read the article. The story was about the mysterious death of Ted and Adrianna. Shaken by the event, he discarded the newspaper into the trash can.

Dr Sutherland entered the waiting room. She headed toward Priest Hamilton. Sensing something happening, Sister Lawrence opened her eyes from her deep prayer and stood.

"I'm Dr Sutherland. Sister Beatrice is in my care. Would you please follow me?"

Dr Sutherland led them through a door that connected to a narrow corridor with numbered doors on each sides of the aisle. They stopped at a door marked number five. Entering the room, Dr Sutherland sat behind her desk.

"Please have a seat," invited the doctor.

Sister Lawrence was nervous as she anticipated something terrible. Priest Hamilton sat next to her facing the doctor. His face showed no sign of emotions.

"I don't mean to alarm you." Dr Sutherland picked up a document from her neatly arranged desk. "There is something sort of phenomenal happening."

"Please doctor, explain."

"Yes, yes of course." She seemed unsure of how to explain her findings. "I examined Sister Beatrice after her abduction. Her virginity was still intact, meaning her hymen was, I mean is still intact. There is no sign of penetration. She is now pregnant. There aren't any DNA samples to obtain until the embryo is developed."

"Are you sure about this?" asked the priest.

"Quite sure. I have to admit I am a woman of science, but there is no explanation to this abnormality."

"Do you know what this means?" suggested Sister Lawrence. "It means you are right Priest Hamilton. Sister Beatrice's disappearance was miraculous and this proves it. Maybe that's why she doesn't recall any of the details. Maybe it's because of its divine nature. Just like we don't remember being born." Sister Lawrence stood excitedly. "This is an Immaculate Conception, the second coming of Christ through a virgin. It's just as it is written in Matthew, chapter 24."

"Can we see her now?" asked Priest Hamilton.

"Yes."

17

Sister Beatrice was carefully taken out of the church vehicle and placed in a wheelchair. She was pushed toward a massive audience. The media was stationed on the sidewalk and steps of the church. Sister Beatrice unintentionally became an overnight sensation. The network ratings accelerated as the days passed with the coverage of her ordeal. A few media giants were negotiating to make a reality television show of the entire event as it unfolded.

"Sister Beatrice is it true you are pregnant?" asked a reporter from an independent network.

Sister Beatrice remained quiet as she was being propelled by Priest Hamilton. Another news correspondent placed a microphone in front of Priest Hamilton.

"People are say this is another Immaculate Conception, a

parallel to Jesus' birth through a virgin. So in all actuality could this be the Second Coming of Jesus?"

Priest Hamilton stopped. "I believe all things are possible through Christ." He continued onward into the church.

From that day forward, news and camera crews were permanently stationed in front of the church. It was an effort to capture exclusive footage and interviews.

***

Dr Sutherland exited the hospital into a sea of media personnel. She couldn't believe how fast the story had snowballed. A microphone was placed in her path.

"Dr Sutherland, it is said that you examined Sister Beatrice after her abduction and prior to her pregnancy. You were quoted saying that Sister Beatrice is still a virgin. Can you give us a few words?"

"I'm sorry to say that is classified information. It is called patient-doctor confidentiality." She continued onward toward her vehicle. As she drove, her mind contemplated. *'I don't know what's going on but there's has to be a logical explanation to this.'* Although she was raised religious, she wasn't fanatical about it. Studying science made her belief system dwindle.

18

Detective Hall sat in his office going over documents that were long overdue to being solved. With his sleeves rolled to his elbow, tie loosened, and the top button of his shirt unfastened, he examined the files on his desk. A knock came to the door.

"Enter!"

The head of a pleasant looking woman peered into the room. It was his secretary. Her caramel complexion, wide nose, and puffy lips were pleasant to the eyes.

"Mrs Jacobs! What can I do for you?"

The rest of her body materialized through the threshold. Her body was shapely. She wore a black, skirt suit with a beige, rayon blouse. Her perfume was delectable to his senses. Detective Hall enjoyed working with Mrs Jacob. Her demeanor was always pleasant.

"I have the background information you requested on the murder-suicide case."

"Thank you Irene. I was just thinking about it." She handed the documents to the detective. She turned and exited the office without saying another word.

Detective Hall removed the documents from two manila envelopes. He studied the female's profile first. The information revealed her name was Adrianna Houghton amongst other personal data. His eyes scanned the criminal history section of the folder. *'Hmm, she's squeaky clean.'* Next was the male victim's profile. Doing a comparison study, Detective Hall noticed the two were employed at the same company. *'Okay, a job-related love affair. 'What made it go bad?'* He wrote those exact words on a pad on the desk and circled it. The detective spotted an inconsistency in the male victim's personal data. *What have we here Mr Conwell?'* He read how the deceased man had an origin that started in South Carolina. Detective Hall had an idea.

After investigating the victim's place of employment, Detective Hall headed across the bridge to Manhattan. The New York Public Library was one of the largest in the country. The building was massive with high vaulted ceilings. Dated architectural designs were throughout the structure, including massive marble columns were numerous. Detective Hall headed toward a section designated for microfilm. He sat at a large table that held a microfilm machine. He pressed the selection menu to read the periodicals. He typed in Beaufort, South Carolina. He used the search engine by typing in the name Ted Conwell. Newspaper articles began strolling down the screen. One particular caption caught his attention. The caption read

BISHOP SEXUALLY ABUSED TWO PARISHIONERS.

Detective Hall continued reading the story. *'Hmm, very interesting.'* He continued strolling. He stopped at another article that was was sixteen years later. The caption read **CHURCH FIRE COLLAPSE BUILDING/BISHOP BODY FOUND INSIDE.** Detective Hall was intrigued by the story and the way it was described as being questionably arson related. Finished with the research, he headed back to the office.

Just as Detective Hall was about to hang up his coat on the rack, the telephone rang. Halting his movement, he picked up the receiver.

"Hello?" He listened to the caller. "Dr Sutherland, what an unsuspected surprise. What can I do for you?" He listened. "Okay, I can be there within a half hour." More silence. "Okay, bye." Placing the receiver back on the cradle, Detective Hall headed out of the door.

19

Priest Hamilton opened the service to a record number crowd. There was standing room only. The ventilation system strained to accommodate all of the people that came to hear and witness the miraculous phenomena. Camera crews belonging to the medias were posted outside of the church. Some were allowed inside. Traffic buildup in the area was profound. The entire street area was nothing more than a giant parking lot.

"...so as we are here today witnessing the miraculous event taking place. Each and everyone here knows that deep inside their psyche a prophecy is being fulfilled. You want to be part of God's work. But, since it is only living in you cognitively, I am going to manifest it in words. Yes, this is the Second Coming of Christ. Are you ready? Are you prepared? Have you done everything in your power to prepare for his arrival? As it is said in Matthew 23:33. You snakes, you generation of vipers, how will you escape the damnation of hell? As you can see we need to expand this facility for preparations. It says in Deuteronomy 14:22. Be sure to set aside a tenth of all that your fields produce each year. Proverbs 3:9-10 says. Honor the Lord with your wealth, with the first fruits of all your crops, then your barns will be filled to overflowing and your vats will brim over with new wine. That is the word of God. When the nuns pass the offering baskets, please give to God so that He may give onto you." Priest Hamilton stepped away from the podium. He waved toward the audience and the cameras as he exited the room. Everyone felt the passionate sermon. Soon after, the nuns began passing around the offering baskets.

Priest Hamilton sat in his office later in the day going over the financial reports. He was happy with the results of the church's income. The results of its gradual increase was gratifying. A knock came to the door.

"Please, come in."

Sister Beatrice entered the rectory. Dressed in clergy attire, her face held a worried expression. Priest Hamilton placed his pen on the desk. He gazed into Sister Beatrice's eyes. "Why the gloomy look? You should be overjoyed that you're the chosen one."

She cowered. "I know…" She took a seat opposite the desk facing the priest. "It's just with all the media coverage, it has me on edge. What if it's not the child everyone thinks it's suppose to be? What then?"

"Have faith dear child. Everything will be revealed in time." He stood and approached Sister Beatrice. He placed a hand on her shoulder. "Do you see all the attention that this has attracted? These people are with you. They believe and will support you."

"I'm afraid." She gazed into Carl's eyes with her liquid brown eyes.

"Don't be, everything is going well. Now get some rest."

***

Junior's restaurant is a famous establishment located in the downtown section of Brooklyn. The restaurant has remained at the same location for 100 years. They were widely known for their famous cheesecakes. The interior held three sections. There was a dining area, a counter service, and a lounge area. The atmosphere was always pleasant, upscale, and casual.

Dr Sutherland and Detective Hall sat in the dining area. Tasty seafood platters were placed on the table. They felt the undercurrent with the situation but they remained professional.

"There is something strange going on with the clergy case," said Dr Sutherland. Her black hair radiated in the soft lighting of the restaurant. She picked up her glass and took a sip.

"Funny you should say that. I also have an inkling about this case." Detective Hall stared into the doctor's liquid brown eyes. He fought hard not to show he was mesmerized by her beauty.

"As you know, I've checked Sister Beatrice after the abduction. There's no logical explanation to this. That is what worries me.

Don't get me wrong, I'm fine with religion. It's just that most things have a scientific explanation."

"I've been researching some things. It seems that a recent murder-suicide case led me to South Carolina. I've also began a research on the priest. As suspected it led to a dead end. Somehow, I believe that…" He held up a hand as a gesture. "I don't know why, but that his past goes in that direction."

"I don't understand the similarities?"

"Right now all I have is theories and vague thoughts. As I dig deeper, I'll let you know more." He stared into her eyes. "So does this mean we're officially networking on this together?"

Dr Sutherland smiled. "I guess you could say that."

"Doctor…"

"Call me Marlene."

"Marlene in time you will find that I'm a very diligent person. I won't stop until I get results."

Marlene recognized the innuendo in his phrase and the undercurrent of its message. "Is that so?" She blushed at the thought. "So where is Mrs Hall?"

"You can call me Doug. There's no one in my life at this time. My job seems to kill all the opportunities that came along in the past. Reason being is…" He sighed deeply. "Have you ever saw a child so fear-stricken because someone had killed her mother in front of her? Well, I'm persistent to catching that criminal. Night and day. Just as I'm with this nun's abduction."

Marlene felt the dedication and the seriousness in his voice and words. *He's caring and I like that. Definitely serious natured. Another asset.*

Take it easy Marlene.'

"So what made you become a doctor?"

"I grew up in Chicago's south side. Coming from a single parent household, my mother worked hard to send me to school which wasn't nearly enough. Luckily, my grade achievements awarded me a full scholarship which helped me to finish school."

"That's a wonderful story. You should be proud."

They continued conversing. Laughter filled the air at times. The two became comfortable with one another. As the evening progressed, Detective Hall paid the bill and drove Dr Sutherland home.

EIGHT

WEEKS

LATER

20

Priest Carl Hamilton listened to the controversy within his church and the actual teachings of the scriptures. There were so-called theologian scholars refuting the claims about his ministry and the Second Coming of Jesus to the All Saint Church. The pope was notified, being that it was thought to be a Catholic denomination. The Cardinal had no record of Priest Hamilton. Carl smiled at all the publicity he was generating. *'It couldn't be better.* He turned off the television and went outside of the newly acquired building. It was located in Macon, Georgia. In the Monroe County Township. The place was situated on a 100 acre spread. It was donated by well-wishers trying to get in good with Jesus as they saw it. To Carl, the gift couldn't have come at a better time because the original building was at capacity. To his thinking, going south meant more African-Americans, and a more diverse following.

Pine trees mixed with cherry and acacia trees gave the area a serene appearance. Carl walked along a pathway that led to an open space of tents. As far as the eyes could see, tents sprang up. At the top of a hill, Priest Hamilton positioned a podium. The media coverage brought spectators from around the country. They all came to witness the childbirth. Some followers liquidated all of their worldly possessions to be in favor with the upcoming event. It was bigger than anything Carl could have imagined. *'Every dollar donated is non-taxable. Good old American tax codes. Steal from the poor and give to the rich.'* Carl thought of the scheme as a game of chest. He lined all of his pieces up in exact positions as he awaited to strike. The thought made him think of Sister Beatrice.

"Come in."

Priest Hamilton entered the house that was located adjacent to the main building. It too was a lavish gift offered by a local construction firm. The house was a ranch style home with two bedrooms, two bathrooms, large living room, and a sizable kitchen. The entire house was completely furnished in modern decor. They figured that since Sister Beatrice was young, she would enjoy the living arrangements.

"I just stopped by to see if you needed anything."

Sister Beatrice was sitting on a sofa in the living room. Her narrow facial features now displayed puffiness. Her stomach protruded. She was now in her mid-term of pregnancy. Sister Beatrice used the arm of the sofa to support herself to stand. Everything that was once an easy task became more difficult to perform as the days passed.

"Yes, I need for Sister Lawrence to take over my class of the third graders." She entered into the kitchen. Opening the refrigerator, she withdrew a jar of pickles and chocolate spread.

"You needn't worry about that." Watching her devour the chocolate dipped pickles fascinated him.

She tried to speak with a mouthful of food. The words came out mumbled. "I don't know what it is…" She chewed some more. I just can't get enough of this…" She gestured with the pickle in her hand.

"I am glad that you can find enjoyment in something." Priest Hamilton stood and headed toward the exit. "Oh yeah, by the way. I'm going to assign one of the sisters to stay with you during this period."

Sister Beatrice continued eating. She nodded her approval as Priest Hamilton exited. *'Oh well, I will be glad when this ordeal is over.'*

Outside, the perimeter of the compound was overflowing with activity. Seemingly, anti-religious groups were exercising their First Amendment rights to freedom of speech by protesting the acclaims of the All Saint Church doctrines. Some of the church followers stood their grounds in front.

News reporters were on the scene. The local police were called in to defuse the heightened tension of the situation. Priest Hamilton looked over at the commotion. He read some of the signs carried by the protesters. He headed toward the podium to began his service.

FIVE

MONTHS

LATER

21

Sister Beatrice was now being given special care. Round the clock teams were assigned to take care of her needs. From hospice to prenatal diagnostic testing was constantly being monitored. The fetus growing inside of her was taking form. The display was happening internally and externally. The male fetus was identified with the use of sonogram. He could be seen making a fist. Frown lines were detected. Positioned in the downward position, the baby was almost ready to see the physical world.

Sister Beatrice felt the pangs associated with childbearing as she moved about the house. She walked into the nursery, the area where the extraordinary baby's room was erected. The room held the ambiance of royalty. The color purple was elegantly displayed throughout the color scheme. It was mixed with the color gold. Authentic precious metals such as silver and gold artifacts were displayed around the room. The distinctive aroma of Frankincense filled the air space with a keen odor. The scene was replicated as described in the Bible as the First Coming of Jesus. Beatrice sat on the bed. *'Why me? What do I know about raising a child?'* She said a silent prayer.

Commotion filled the room from the open window in the bedroom. The sound interrupted her meditative thoughts. Sister Beatrice peered out of the window. She gazed at the sea of tents. She saw massive crowds of people holding signs and shouting slogans. They were too far in distance for her to distinguish any features.

***

Demonstrators squared off at the front gate of the compound. State troopers were there to keep the peace. A muslim faction called Mahallah were dressed in middle-eastern, religious garbs. They were upset over the church's depiction of the God being born to a Catholic nun. They felt the notion was disrespectful and blasphemy.

Another religious group of men called Hebrew Israelites were dressed in radical combat clothing. They also argued the claim, but their understanding was different. Their dispute declared no way Christ could have come from a caucasian nun. That the entire principles of the scriptures were contrast to those opinions. One of the African-American leaders stood on a makeshift platform with a bullhorn in front of his mouth.

"Listen, do not be fooled. Listen to what is said in the scriptures about the description of the Son of Man. It says in Revelation 1:14-15. *'His head and his hairs were white like wool, as white as snow; and his eyes were as a flame of fire. And his feet like unto fine brass, as if they burned in furnace; and his voice as the sounds of many waters.'* From all the ethnic groups on the planet, what race of people closely resemble that description of having wool-like hair? The Black race. There you have it! Bronze describe a man of color. If his feet were bronze, the rest of his body was the same. There's no way are we to believe the second coming will be in the form of a blue-eyed devil. We will not accept that." The crowd screamed. Some for and against the analogy of the statement.

Inside the compound, Priest Hamilton had just finished his sermon. Afterward, the passing of tithe offerings became a huge event. It took more manpower and time to complete. Miles of tents were erected on the grounds. Thousands of people liquidated all of their worldly possessions to be accepted.

Priest Hamilton had to used a larger staff to run the church operations. He sat in his office with ten clergy members standing around a large rectangular wooden table counting the proceeds of the service. Cash machines were utilized to make the process more efficient. Sounds of cash fluttering from the cash counters were pronounce. Adding machines were also implemented. The overall ambience of the scene spelled business. If not for the staff wearing cleric outfits, the two different worlds of business and religion would be hard to tell apart.

Priest Hamilton smiled inwardly. He wanted to hide his thoughts. Outwardly, he kept a peaceful disposition. *'Lets keep it together. You are almost there…'*

22

Detective Hall awakened with an idea. As he prepared to leave the house, he picked up the morning newspaper. It was laid on the doorstep. He glanced at the headline caption. He was intrigued. He took the newspaper along with him to his vehicle. The drive to the office was easy. No traffic existed.

Detective Hall entered the office. He sat behind his desk to read the caption story. The story was about Priest Hamilton and how the church had flourished beyond imagination. The great controversy it created was astounding. *'Something is not quite right. I aim to find out what that is.'*

Detective Hall rested during the flight from New York City to Beaufort County, South Carolina. A taxicab took him to the place requested. An old burned and abandoned church stood in ruins. A wooden fence enclosed the area from passersby. It was a bad remembrance and an eyesore. A small padlock was the only security measure in place that kept the detective from his investigative research. Within minutes he was inside.

The church was charred. Nothing was recognizable. Detective Hall sifted through the debris. The act bore no fruits. *The trail here is cold.* He headed toward the place where the questionable deaths occurred.

A 'For Sale' sign was pitched in the front yard of an Old Georgian styled house. Before entering the house another idea struck Detective Hall. He knocked on the door of a neighbor. The door was opened by a woman in her mid 50's. She had blonde hair that was shoulder length. It was obviously a wig. Her face displayed age lines and skepticism. She stood at the door. Her blue eyes peered at the stranger.

"I'm sorry to bother you. I'm Detective Hall. I am investigating the killings of Mrs Marteni and her son." He displayed his identification document.

"But it says here that you are a New York City detective. You don't have jurisdiction here."

"Yes, that may be true in some sense, but it is believed that one of the priest in question might have committed the crime and fled afterward."

She looked out of the door to get a better reading on the situation. She stepped back into the house to allow the detective entrance. "Please have a seat. Would you like something to drink? I just made a pitcher of lemonade."

"Yes, that would be fine Mrs…"

"Parsons." She went into the kitchen, leaving the detective in the living room.

Detective Hall studied the decor in the room. He noticed the house was well organized and neat. Pictures of family members hung on the mantle. Mrs Parsons returned from the kitchen carrying a sterling silver serving tray. Upon the tray was a pitcher of lemonade, two glasses, and a few pastries.

"I hope you like it, I made them myself." She served the detective. She placed the tray on the table and sat next to the detective. "What can I do for you?"

"I need information on the Marteni family." Detective Hall placed his glass on the table.

"They've been murdered!" she exclaimed emotionally.

"Who would want to kill them?"

"The same ones responsible for killing the bishop. You see, there was a scandal. I should know, I used to attend that church. In fact, everyone around these parts used to attend there because of its strong history in the area. Anyway, before the mishap took place, Karen came to me saying that she was going public with the fact that her son was molested by two priest at that church. She first went to the bishop and demanded that they be ousted from the congregation. The next thing, the bishop was dead. So was Mrs Marteni and her son." Tears flowed down Mrs Parsons' face.

"What were the two priest's names?"

"Ted Conwell and Carl Brandon."

The names mentioned sent a shiver of excitement down the detective's spine. He'd read the story on the fate of Ted Conwell in New York. *'His partner must be Priest Hamilton. I've got to make sure.'* He focused his attention to Mrs Parsons who was obviously shaken by the story. "Mrs Parsons…" Detective Hall stood. "You have been a big help and a gracious host. I think I have enough information for now. If I need anything else I'll call you if that would be okay."

"Okay, no problem. I hope you catch the culprits responsible for these heinous acts."

"I aim to ma'am."

Detective Hall's next stop was the Beaufort County sheriff office. The building was historic as the town itself. It was a wooden, one level, structure that was built from its original material. A newly, prefabrication was added recently. It held the confinement quarters in the rear.

Detective Hall entered the building to find a small interior that was cluttered. There were three desks spaced apart. Bulletins were placed on the walls in some areas. There were also photographs of the town's sporting events on display. Large ceiling fans rotated in efforts to circulate the dry, humid, air in the room.

Detective Hall one officer occupying a desk. *'Maybe the others are out on patrol.'* He approached the desk.

"Hi, I'm Detective Hall…" He displayed his identification document. "I would like to know about a case that happened here some time ago."

The desk sergeant looked at the stranger dressed in a suit and tie. He studied the man's credentials. "You're a long way from home…"

He stood with an outstretched hand. The detective received the welcoming. The desk sergeant was a huge man with a firm handshake. His brown hair and walrus styled mustache gave him a distinguish appearance. The detective sized him up instantly. His trained eyes summed the sheriff to be about 230 pounds, six feet, and slightly overweight.

"I'm Sergeant Wilroy. What can I do for you? Have a seat."

Detective Hall sat directly in front of the sergeant. "Is there any information about the strange fire and the death of the bishop?"

The sergeant studied the detective's demeanor. "What's it to you?"

"I know about the molestation charges. I know about two priest that were victims. I think it's safe to say the fire was a coverup to a murder. One of the priest landed in my neck of the woods…"

"Which one is that?" The sergeant displayed interest.

Detective Hall retrieved a note pad from his jacket. Turning the page, he read off a name. Although he knew the name from memory, he wanted it to be viewed as thoroughness. The detective realized that some people like to know they have valuable contributions. It was a strong attribute for the detective to notice details. "Ted Conwell." He noticed the name had an effect on the sheriff's demeanor.

"Yes, he was a priest at the church around that time. Yes, you are right. It was a nasty scandal that drained this town emotionally. So do you have him apprehended? We'd like to question him."

"So would we, only he's dead." The sheriff seemed bewildered from the statement. "There were two of them we believe."

"Yes, there was his partner that we've never been able to locate. His name is Carl Brandon."

"Carl Brandon." Detective Hall interjected simultaneously as the sheriff. "Yes, I am quite aware. Is there a photograph of him anywhere?"

"Sure." He stood and walked over to a file cabinet in the rear of the office. Retrieving a folder, he returned to his desk. The sergeant rifled through the contents. He produced a glossy eight by ten color photograph of both priests at a church outing. The two were shown giving food to the young children.

"Can I have a copy of this?"

"You can keep it. So do you have a lead on Carl?"

"It's too premature to tell. I will tell you this. As soon as we know something, I will personally notify you of the actions taken."

"Thank you detective."

23

As the days grew near for Sister Beatrice's childbearing to reach its final stage, so did the massive crowds and the many different cults grew outside. The media was responsible for getting the news out all over the globe of the miraculous event. Every television and radio network was tuned in on this phenomenon. It was the biggest thing since the World Trade Tower disaster. Foreign visitors began assembling with the masses. The federal government became concerned and began infiltrating the masses. They were disguised as different ethnic groups. Disputes began to spring up all over the country. The unrest stemmed from the diverse interpretations of biblical decrees by different religious sects. State troopers and national guards were called in. The entire world watched.

Television and radio ratings soared.

Sister Beatrice sat in the living room with Sister Lawrence. They were watching the news captions of the compound. Tired of viewing the story, Sister Beatrice used the remote to turn off the television.

Sister Lawrence witnessed the agitation in Sister Beatrice's demeanor. "I've read on different accounts that even Mary had to be taught first in order to teach her baby Jesus."

"Yes, I've heard that he practically came out of the womb talking…" She held her face in her hands in frustration. "I don't know if I can deal with that."

"Sister Beatrice look at me…" Sister Lawrence waited to get her attention. "You'll never have to be alone with this. The entire world is at your disposal. Just look outside." Sister Beatrice was guided toward the window. "They're here for you and your baby."

Sister Beatrice viewed the massive amount of people that took up refuge in the area. They were there to witness the childbirth. She was touched by Sister Lawrence's words of encouragement. The softness in her phonetical tone was touching. The two returned to the sofa.

"I'll tell you what, we have a huge private area in which to walk. Let's go for a stroll. I promise you the air will be good for you."

The area was sectioned off to provide privacy. A huge field was gated behind trees in efforts not to disturb the land's natural beauty. They strolled on a blanket of pine needles and acorns. Squirrels cowered around tall oak trees. Large redwood trees blended into the landscaping. Sister Lawrence and Sister Beatrice slowly walked as they enjoyed the beautiful scenery. It was definitely therapeutic for them.

Serenity came from the natural sounds of the animals and birds. The sun emitted rays of iridescence in the sky.

They came upon a brook. It was there they stopped to sit. The afternoon sun was high in the sky. It was positioned directly above them. High noon had approached. Warmth from the rays blanked them as they basked in the glorious splendor.

Sister Beatrice tossed a pebble into the water. She studied the waves as the stone impacted the water. "Sister Lawrence, suppose I did not want to be a nun after this ordeal is over?" She watched her reaction to the question.

"What do you mean? Of course you want to continue being a nun. You are chosen child."

Sister Beatrice gazed at Sister Lawrence. "Suppose I wanted to take my baby elsewhere and live out a normal quiet life?"

"I don't think you realize the people believe you are carrying the Messiah. Where would you find a quiet life?"

"What do you think? Is that what you believe?" Sister Beatrice studied her eyes as she waited for a response.

Sister Lawrence listen to the sincerity in her question. She also sensed the tenseness in Sister Beatrice's demeanor. "I believe you are with the child of God. How else would you be claimed a virgin by the medical authorities and still be pregnant? There is only one parallel story to match yours on the entire planet and that is the birth of Jesus. So you see, this is a prophecy being fulfilled."

Sister Beatrice looked away. Her vision was captured by the still waters. Her mind was in turmoil. She was afraid. More so, she needed privacy.

***

A blue and white tractor-trailer moved away from the compound. The truck held writings on its side panels that read UNITED CHRISTIAN FOUNDATION. A logo attached to the advertisement was a depiction of a fish. The large machine parted the crowd that milled about the rear of the compound. They were mostly paparazzi and reporters staked out on the premises. Some were positioned in trees in efforts to get an exclusive photograph for the tabloids in which they were employed.

Priest Hamilton smiled as the truck made its way down the main road. He sat behind his paper cluttered desk. He was filled with delight at his plan. *'I think this is the biggest event in the world, and I'm responsible for it.'* His mind thought about Ted Conwell. *'If you would have only waited a little longer buddy we would have owned the world together.'*

24

FEDERAL BUREAU OF INVESTIGATION
FRAUD DIVISION/8TH FLOOR
ONE FEDERAL PLAZA
MANHATTAN, NEW YORK

Detective Hall sat in the main conference room with two distinguished gentlemen seated across from him. Both men emitted an air of importance. The two wore dark colored suits. One black the other charcoal gray. Both men wore handmade silk ties. The accessories hung royally around their necks. Having an eye for detail, Detective Hall instantly noticed the contrast between the two men. The gentleman on the left of him had pale, wrinkling skin, gray hair, and was well-groomed. He sat facing Detective Hall from behind a rectangular conference table. His legs were crossed. His title and name was Director Newhart. He ran the division for seven years. His duty was to protect the citizens from white collar criminals. During the years, he saw many different scams employed on innocent people. He hated the ones that targeted the elderly and poor.

The other gentleman was much younger. His complexion was the color of coffee. His nose was wide, his lips protruded. His African-American heritage was prominent in his features. Beneath his suit was a silhouette of his toned body. His wide frame and broad shoulders towered over his co-worker. Assistant Director Greg Porter was among his accolades. He was the go-between man in the field. Before any information worthy of attention was sent to the director, it had to go through him. The two listened to Detective Hall's finding on Carl Brandon, who went by the name Priest Hamilton. The pictures they obtained depicted him exactly.

"If you really think this is a deceptive movement, what do you suppose his true motives are? How do you think it can be accomplished?" asked the director.

"To be honest, I've spent so much time on the trail of identifying the culprit that I haven't had much time to process his motive. One thing I can say for sure, there's a lot of people liquidating their worldly possessions to be in his grace."

"You have a point there," responded Mr Porter. He jotted something onto a small notepad. "Money does seem to be the primary concern."

"Where do you think he'll take the money once he has obtained what he want? He can't keep it all there, it would be unsafe," added the director.

"Upon investigation, I spotted a few United Christian Foundation vehicles moving about the compound."

"I think a global positioning system satellite over that area would be in order. I'll make the necessary calls. Also, some ears on the compound to listen better would be suffice. We have to find out what they're planning. We must know if they're working with a foreign government to dethrone ours," stated the director.

"We already have men infiltrated on the ground. I'll see what kind of intel they've accumulated," stated Mr Porter.

***

Detective Hall returned to his office. He felt elated with being able to get the federal authorities involved. His merriment caused him to think of Dr Sutherland. Marlene was a bright spot in his once socially secluded existence. Although they were seeing more of one another, it was nothing to the extent they would have liked. The case, just as the others, always seemed to take center stage in his life. *'Not this time. I will not let her get away.'* Detective Hall picked up the telephone and began dialing. It was answered on the second ring.

Dr Marlene Sutherland had just finished doing a bypass on an elderly man. The operation was successful. She exited the operating room feeling optimistic about life. Entering her office she heard the telephone ring. She snatched up the receiver on the second ring. She was delighted to hear the voice on the other end. The conversation continued pass the preliminary pleasantries to business at hand.

"So, was your trip revealing?"

"Yes, in fact it's the reason I called. It turns out the priest is masquerading as another clergyman. I also have the cooperation of the federal government. There may come a time when I can only trust you for personal diagnosis. Will that be all right with you?"

A moment of silence pursued. "Yes, that will be fine. What's next?"

"Us." There was confidence in his voice. Dr Sutherland was caught by surprise at the answer. She smiled. "I figured we could spend a quiet evening dining."

"That sound splendid. What do you have in mind?"

"Something casual and laid back. It will be a surprise. I'll pick you up at seven."

"That sounds wonderful. I'll be waiting, bye." Dr Sutherland disconnected the call. She was having a foreboding inkling. At first, she thought it was due to something work related. She thought of the telephone call she just received. *There's a few things that need to be done before he gets here.'* She placed on her jacket and headed out of the door.

25

Carl Hamilton sat in the confines of his master bedroom. The enclosure was well decorated with fine wood and Italian marble. He switched off the television set and continued staring at the blank screen. His mind recollected tidbits from his past.

Images of his father loomed into the center of his mind's eye. *"Didn't I tell you that taking what is not yours will only cause you pain?" stated his father. His dad was a large burly man about five feet, nine inches. He weighed 185 pounds. The two favored one another in facial descriptions such as eyes, cheeks, mouth, and hair. Carl was eight years old at the time. He had taken a cookie from a jar in the kitchen without permission when his father walked into the room. His father had backed him into a corner screaming at the top of his lungs. Carl was afraid, he dropped the cookie onto the floor. A right hand from his father landed young Carl onto the cold, linoleum floor. A slap from his father stung the side of his face. Carl cowered from the onslaught of attacks from his father. His mother rushed into the room to stop her husband from attacking the boy. His father had already taken off his leather belt and began to hit Carl. The boy was terrified. His eyes were wide open and his body shivered.*

"Harry! Please stop! You're going to kill him. He's too young..." She was propelled backward by a forceful push from his strong arm. The force was so great and the momentum so intense, she fell over a chair and landed on the floor near the stove.

"Don't you tell me how to raise my boy!" he shouted. His eyes were slits from anger. His attention was adverted to Carl. "Now get up! Go read your bible and find the part that talks about stealing and its punishment. It's nothing compared to what I'm doing. Now go!"

Reluctant to leave, he watched helplessly as his father snatched his mother from the floor as if she was weightless. "I told you never to interfere with me when I'm chastising my son." He pulled her down the stairs toward the basement.

Wide-eyed with terror, Carl watched helplessly. He couldn't move. It was as if his body was no longer in his control. He wanted to scream but his vocal apparatus seemed temporarily impaired. Fear associated with guilt overwhelmed him. He knew she wouldn't have been in that predicament if it wasn't for him. Tears flowed down his face as he helplessly watched his father drag his screaming mother down to the basement. It was a place he was always forbidden to enter.

From that day forward, he never saw his mother again. When asked about her whereabouts, he would receive the same answer.

"Your mother was weak. She abandoned us forever." The reply was repetitious to his questioning. At that moment, a deep torment of emotional pain surrounded the young boy's perception of life. 'One day I'll get even with you for taking my mother away from me.' thought Carl.

KNOCK! KNOCK! KNOCK!

The raps on the door was forceful. The disturbance was enough to return Carl from his reverie to the present moment.

Sister Lawrence entered the room hastily. She didn't wait for permission to enter. "I think it's time. Sister Beatrice's water just broke." The two hurried out of the room toward Sister Beatrice's quarters.

Priest Carl Hamilton rushed into Sister Beatrice's room to find people around the bed. Three nuns were attending to her. The resident doctor was monitoring her vital signs with a digital graph machine. The doctor saw Carl enter. Carl sensed the tension in the room. Sister Beatrice's screams confirmed his belief. The doctor approached.

"There seems to be a problem. She's hemorrhaging and I can't stop the bleeding." The doctor was an elder man with white hair and thick, white eyebrows. He walked with a limp. He wore horn-rimmed eyeglasses on his slender nose. The doctor carried a stethoscope around his neck.

"What do you recommend we do? asked Carl. He gazed at the doctor. His attention went to Sister Beatrice as she remained in bed. She grimaced in pain.

"As I've said from the beginning, she should have been in the hospital where the care would be greater."

"Are you sure there's nothing you can do for her here? Have you noticed the massive mob that this pregnancy has attracted?"

"I understand your dilemma, but I think her safety outweighs anything else."

Carl studied the doctor's demeanor. "You're absolutely correct."

His attention went toward Sister Lawrence. "Call for an ambulance!"

"Yes sir."

Two medical technicians inched their way through the massive crowd. The emergency lights on top of the vehicle flashed as the siren wailed in efforts to gain footage. The crowd sensed the urgency and allowed the vehicle through. The intrusion of medical assistance caused concern for the onlookers and media crews. Reporters could be seen jotting down the information on the side panels of the emergency vehicle.

The vehicle finally made it to the front of the church. The medical technicians rushed into the building. One carried a collapsible gurney.

They found Sister Beatrice in distress and pain. They methodically went into action. One medical technician was a thin, tall man with black hair and dark eyes. He began taking a reading of her vitals. The other technician, an African-American man, went to the source of the hemorrhage.

"Where does it hurt you sister?" asked the technician as he continued taking reading of her vitals.

Sister Beatrice's voice was raspy, her tone was low. "B-Bottom of my stomach…" She grimaced in pain.

The African-American, medical technician, saw the source of the problem. "My guess is she's not expanding quick enough." He reached into his case and retrieved a syringe and a vial of clear liquid. "I'm going to…"

"N-No sedatives, no drugs," requested Sister Beatrice.

The technician eyed his partner, then Sister Beatrice. He returned the items back into the case. "We better hurry and get you to the hospital."

Sister Beatrice was fastened onto the gurney. She was quickly wheeled to the waiting vehicle. A white sheet was placed over her entire body to cover her identity. It was a safety precaution. The crowd watch the gurney being placed into the ambulance. They crowd began to panic. Screams and chants were loud.

"She's dead!" shouted someone in the crowd.

"They're taking away the virgin!" shouted another agitator.

"Stop them!"

The crowd became frantic. Hysteria took control of the masses. As the emergency vehicle tried to make its exit, it was blocked by the angry crowd. Some tried to open the rear doors, while others banged on the passenger and driver side windows. In their cognizance, they were attempting to free the captive Sister Beatrice. The crowd seized the van and began rocking it from side to side.

Inside the rear compartment of the vehicle, Sister Lawrence and Sister Beatrice were frightened. The technicians were also bewildered.

"W-What are we gonna do?" asked one technician to the other.

"Don't panic! Get on the radio and call for police assistance. There are police and national guards on the compound."

The medical technician did as he was told. Afterward, they waited. A stone impacted the windshield and shattered the glass. The tempered safety protection glass remained intact.

"What's happening? Why are they doing this?" asked Sister Lawrence. She was obviously hysterical.

"Just remain calm!" retorted the driver. Noise from a fist banged on the exterior of the van. The sound was startling and added to the urgency of the matter.

Suddenly, the van began to tilt. The medical equipment that was fastened to the walls and shelves began dislodging from their stationary positions. Sister Lawrence was afraid as she held onto a post that was mounted on the wall of the van. She looked over to see that Sister Beatrice was in a silent prayer as she held onto her rosary beads.

At that instant, as if her prayer was answered, the ambulance ceased its violent eruption. Everyone inside the vehicle was in awe and taken by surprise at the sudden change. The nuns believed it was their prayer responsible for the change. Sister Beatrice believed it was the passage she read in Matthew chapter 18:20: *For where two or three are gathered together in my name, there I am in the midst of them.*

The medical technicians believed it was the call to the dispatcher requesting assistance. Through shattered glass, everyone saw state troopers and national guardsmen converge on the scene. Order was being restored. After some time in delay, they were permitted to continue on their path. Silence ensued for the rest of the trip. Everyone reveled in the past experience. The perilous situation took a toll on everyone. They all gave thanks to what they believed in.

***

Carl gazed out of the window as Sister Beatrice and Sister Lawrence boarded the ambulance. He smiled inwardly. *'Perfect! You're just about there.'* He had stayed back purposely as the decision to call for an ambulance was made. He would have liked the opportunity to collect the rest of the day's tithes, but he knew time had arrived. He also realized that he would have to react soon.

Carl watched as the vehicle moved forward. He witnessed the agitated crowd converge on the ambulance. He used that precise moment to react. Everyone in the room ran to the window to see the commotion.

Carl used that opportunity to ease out of the room. He headed down the corridor to another room at the far end. Inside was another room similar to the first. It was used for guest lodging. Inside, he went to work on the other part of his plan. Quickly, he entered the bathroom area and began stripping out of his priestly garments. He began cutting his hair and shaving. He dyed his hair black afterward. Carl applied a skin toner to his body to darken his appearance. Next, he changed into secular garbs he'd secretly purchased months ago.

Thirty minutes later, Carl resembled a completely different person. There was no sign of his former appearance. He gazed into the bathroom mirror at his facial hair disguise. He wore what appeared to be a light beard with a connecting goatee. A pair of tinted eyeglasses covered his eyes. He placed on a cotton jacket and adorned a sports cap. Carl headed out of the door. He hesitated as a thought occurred. Carl reentered the room to retrieve the camera left in the closet. He slung it around his neck with a media identification card attached to the lapel. He exited through the rear entrance and blended with the group of news reporters.

26

A restaurant called The View is located on the top floor of the Marriot hotel. The establishment resided on Broadway and 45th Street in Manhattan. The dining experience is encased around a large window that wraps around the entire establishment. Business hours were noon to six in the morning. It was famous for its lunch and dinners. The main attraction to the restaurant was its extraordinary view of New York City's skyline. The entire restaurant rotated slowly. In doing so, a complete view of the skyline was prominent. A complete revolution took about an hour. The decor was tastefully arranged. The lighting was soft and the ambiance was pleasant.

Dr Marlene Sutherland and Detective Hall sat at a booth table enjoying a delicious meal. The meal consisted of Pasta e fagioli soup, oven roasted leg of lamb in a red wine sauce, spinach ravioli and tomato sauce. The meal was flavored to perfection. There was cheese-filled ravioli with creamed escarole sauce, sautéed Swiss chard with cannelloni beans. When the meal was brought to the table it was a sight to behold. Everything looked delightful. Doug noticed that the leg of lamb had been deboned. The roast was then rolled, tied, and marinated overnight. The flavorful meat was tender and easy to slice. A smooth, white, aromatic wine accompanied the meal.

Conversation and laughter came with ease. The city lights illuminated outside the window. It displayed an abundance of lights and an iridescence of colors. The soft lighting inside, along with the white wine, caused Marlene to giggle.

"…and the patient came up to me and asked can he borrow…" She discontinued her sentence. She was taken aback at the background in the restaurant.

Doug looked behind to see what had spooked her. He couldn't detect anything out of the ordinary. He turned to face her. "What's wrong?"

"I don't know. Just a minute ago there was an old fashion piano over there in the center of the room. Now it's replaced with a replica of a 1950's telephone booth." She looked on perplexed.

Doug started laughing at the notion. Immediately he knew what she was referring to because it happened to him on his first visit.

"What is so funny?" Marlene became self-conscience.

Doug regained his composure. "I'm not laughing at you. I am laughing with you. I experienced the same thing my first visit here.

You see the area over there?" He gestured with his finger toward where she was referring to. "That area too has a slow rotating floor. So as time passes the scenery changes, just like the view."

Marlene felt slightly embarrassed. "I'm sorry for being so snappy."

"Apology accepted. Now that we've eaten, I want to show you something else."

'I hope it isn't one of these hotel rooms here in the building.'

A yellow medallion taxicab stopped off at South Street and 33rd Street. It was a huge heliport. They exited the vehicle into the sounds of loud engines and rotor blades spinning and whirling wind. Marlene had to hold onto her purse tightly. Taking her by the small of her arm, Doug escorted her to a burgundy and silver helicopter. The pilot greeted them as they entered. The doors were closed automatically. Surprisingly, the interior was quiet and cozy. Inside the cabin resembled that of a limousine. The same amenities were supplied. A bar, television, partition compartment that separated the passengers from the pilot.

Moments later, the aircraft began its ascend. The nocturnal setting allowed them to see the city lights more graphically. Soft music began to play through the speaker system. They sat back and relaxed. Marlene was in awe. She was having a great time. She looked down at the floor to see it was transparent. It gave the illusion of walking on air.

"This is remarkable. You sure know how to impress a lady. How many others have you done this with?"

"None. That is because I've never met anyone like you in my

travels. I feel that as much as I love my work, just for the asking, I would stop for you. That's how I feel about you. I know it's a short time that we've been acquainted, but my feelings for you are real."

"I don't know what to say to that. I am honored you feel that way. I just want us to take it slow so that it we don't descentigrate upon returning to earth. Right now I am defiantly soaring."

"I understand. This is where I'm at. I have to take a trip out of town that is pertaining to the case with the nun. The same one that has the entire country going nuts. When I return I am willing to dedicate my life to being with you. That's if you will have me."

"Shut up and kiss me."

The helicopter touched down on the top of the MGM Casino in Atlantic City, New Jersey. The two danced, gambled, and conversed. Marlene was completely comfortable with Doug. He was gentle and concerning. She wanted to bed him that evening but Doug thought against it. He wanted everything to be perfect when he did. The evening was over. They backtracked their steps and boarded the awaiting helicopter for a return trip home.

27

The medical technicians were surprised to see the magnitude of the crowd assembled in front of Mount Sinai Hospital. Camera crews and reporters jostled for position as the ambulance drove toward the emergency receiving doors. Hospital security was dispatched to the scene. Activists from many factions formulated in front of the hospital. They chanted and held up slogan signs.

The ambulance came to a stop. The security guards met at the entrance. The two emergency medical technicians exited the vehicle and headed toward the rear compartment. As the doors opened, they encountered Sister Lawrence. Sister Beatrice was on the gurney. Although quiet, it was obvious she was in severe pain. She was wheeled into the hospital under police escort. Cameras flashed in the area. Pandemonium ensued at the sight of Sister Beatrice being escorted on the gurney. She was rushed to the seventh floor, a high security section of the hospital. Sister Lawrence was made to wait in another area. She sat quietly in deep prayer.

***

Detective Hall was on the scene in Macon, Georgia. He read about the compound that held All Saint Church in the newspaper. It did nothing to prepare him for the reality of the situation. Tents were pitched as far as the eyes could see. People milled about living out their existence in await for the Second Coming. The scene reminded Detective Hall of the protest called Occupy Wall Street. It was a demonstration that existed in Zuccotti Park in New York City.

Detective Hall used his identification to gain access directly into the church. Inside, clergy people moved about. He stopped a nun as he entered the rectory.

"Excuse me…" He displayed his identification. "I'm here to speak with Sister Beatrice. I am-I mean, I was the investigating officer for Sister Beatrice's abduction in New York."

The nun smiled. She exposed perfect teeth. "I remember you. Did you ever catch the guy?"

"Not yet, but I'm close."

"What can I do for you detective? My name is Sister Spelling."

"I need to talk with Sister Beatrice and Priest Hamilton."

"I'm sorry. Maybe you didn't hear, but Sister Beatrice went into labor today. She was rushed to the hospital. I know for certain that Sister Lawrence accompanied her. I don't know about Priest Hamilton. His rectory is just down the hall and up the stairs to the left."

"Thank you Sister Spelling…" He started on his way. A notion stopped him. "Oh by the way, which hospital did they send Sister Beatrice to?"

"Mount Sinai, downtown."

Detective Hall jotted the information onto a notepad. He continued onward in his search for Priest Hamilton. Following the directions given, Detective Hall came upon a large, thick, mahogany door. He gave it two sharp staccato raps and stood back. No one answered. He repeated the procedure and received the same results.

Detective Hall slowly turned the doorknob counterclockwise. As he entered, he saw the room was immaculate and spotless. The bedding looked to not have been disturbed. He walked slowly around the room carefully not to touch anything. He tried to find something out of place, some sort of inappropriate pattern that would jump out at him and give him a clue to the whereabouts of Priest Hamilton. That didn't happen.

Amid amounting frustration, Detective Hall exited the room. Having an eye for detail, his vision was trained on the thick, plush carpet in the corridor. He was able to see the clean carpet left a set of footprints that led down the corridor from the room he'd just exited. He followed the trail. Stopping at another door that was identical to the first, Detective Hall placed his ear to the wooden door and listened. No sound ensued from the other side. He rapped on the door twice. There was no answer. He tried the doorknob. It was locked. Detective Hall sighed deeply. He retrieved a small black canvas case from his inner jacket pocket. The case contained a set of small carbonized steel picks. He retrieved a pair and began to gain entry.

Within a few seconds he was inside the room. The interior wasn't as large and spacious as the first. The place looked more lived in. Detective Hall saw a discarded priestly robe on the floor. *'Whoever it was must have been in a hurry.'* Continuing his search, he headed into the bathroom. *'Well I'll be damn.'* He'd found a box of hair dye and hair follicles in the sink. Upon further inspection, he saw scissors, comb, and a razor on a stand. Using a towel, he gently placed the items in a the towel. He was careful not to smudge the prints. He exited the room.

Back in the main part of the building, Detective Hall encountered Sister Spelling once again. She was a tall and slender middle-aged woman. Her small lips, rosy cheeks, and reddish-pink freckled face foretold her Irish heritage.

"Did you speak with Priest Hamilton?"

"No I didn't. I would like to have a manila envelope please."

"Sure, right this way." She headed toward the office. Sister Spelling handed the detective an envelope. "Is there anything else?"

"No, no that would be fine. Thank you very much."

***

Detective Hall reached Mount Sinai Hospital. He was astounded by the sea of spectators, media coverage, and the appearance of clergies from different sects and cults. They were all amalgamated into a forceful frenzy. He entered the hospital using his identification. He passed through a wall of security forces. He headed directly for the registration desk. *'I am glad I stopped at the courier office before coming here. Marlene will know what to do. This is a mad house.'*

The receptionist was middle-aged. She was slender. She wore a name plate that read Ms Townsend. Her jet black hair hung at shoulder length. Her fingernails were manicured with French tips. The glossy white tips made a slight tapping noise as she typed on the keyboard. She looked up as the detective approached. The receptionist's complexion was a tad-bit darker than his.

Detective Hall approached the desk. "Hi, my name is Detective Hall. I'm trying to locate Sister Beatrice. I'm told she's in this hospital." He displayed his identification.

She gazed at the identification without handling it. Her eyes connected with the detective's. "It seems the entire world knows. Yeah, she's here. Only you can't get in there to see her. She's in labor and under tight security." The receptionist inched closer to the detective. She began to whisper. "You know everyone thinks she's some kind of saint sent from the scriptures or something. I don't believe it! There's too much hype." She regained her distance. "If you don't believe me you go try to enter on your own. Only, don't say that I didn't warn you. Seventh floor."

***

Marlene signed the delivery receipt for the courier. The box delivered was light in weight. *'Hmm, I wonder who this can be from.'* She inspected the exterior for clues to the sender. Locking the door to her office, Marlene took the package to her desk and began opening it.

The content was wrapped in cellophane. That gave her a clue as to who the sender was. It caused her to smile. *'There may come a time where I can only trust you for personal diagnosis. Will that be all right with you?'* Her mind recollected. She studied the comb, scissors, and hair follicles. She knew exactly what to do. Marlene examined the box for a letter. There was none. She entered the laboratory and began doing an analysis of the items.

28

Carl Hamilton rode on a Greyhound bus along Interstate 16. The vehicle headed west toward Savannah, Georgia. He was adorned in secular clothing. The disguise made it easy for him to blend in with the other commuters. He'd forgot how comfortable regular clothing felt. *'Everything is working as planned.'* The day's events caused exhaustion to permeate his body. He submitted to the sensation. Closing his eyes, his mind drifted to past events. Images of his father loomed with vivid clarity…

'Carl had just returned from church after receiving instructions into the sacred order. After changing from his vestments, he headed into the backyard. For some particular reason, the newly planted plum tree his father planted caused him to wonder.

Returning from the garage with a shovel, Carl began digging around the tree.

After digging a few feet deep, a terrible stench erupted from the cavity. A malodorous stench permeated the area. It was the scent of decaying matter. He knew because he remembered the time he buried his dog and the heavy rain began to exhume the corpse. The odor was the same. He held his breath in efforts to not inhale the putrid odor as he continued to dig deeper into the hard earth. Determined to fulfill his curiosity, Carl worked diligently as sweat cascaded from his body. After 20 minutes into the dig, he stopped abruptly. He witnessed maggots surfacing from underground. Between the unsightly parasites and the awful stench caused Carl to gag. It wasn't the stench that captured his motionless attention, it was what looked like a semi-decomposed hand. It was in a tight balled fist as if it died struggling. His heartbeat raced as adrenaline excreted from his glands. The next thing he noticed, as his mind took longer to process the information, was it changed his perception of life forever. It was a ring. It was the same ring he'd given to his mother. It rested loosely on a boney finger with dried wrinkled flesh. Staring at the ring caused him to recollect the moment.

"Come in son. Why are you standing in the doorway? I'm not going to bite you. At least not yet." She giggled. "And what's that you have behind your back?" His mother's smiled had the effect of brightening his darkest days. She was an attractive woman of Scandinavian descent. Her facial features were well distinguished. The curves and lines were accentuated by her creamy, flawless skin.

Carl entered the room. He exposed the small box that was obscured behind his back. A combination of embarrassment and enthusiasm caused him to smile. Two missing front teeth were exposed. "I bought you something."

"Yeah? What is it?" His mother was intrigued by the gesture. She looked at the box. "It can't be a car. It's too small. Oh! I know, a horse. You bought me a horse. Right?" The statement had its intended effect.

Carl giggled. "It's a ring that I want you to wear. No matter how bad dad treats you, I want you to know that I love you forever. When I grow up I'm going to marry you."

She accepted the ring and placed it on her finger. Tears of endearment fell from her eyes. "It's beautiful son. I will wear it proudly forever."

Seeing the ring caused an indescribable sensation to override his senses. As if in a stupor, young Carl headed back into the house. He was being propelled by anger and revenge.

The pleasant aroma of onions, peppers, and garlic being sautéed was delightful to the senses. Carl was so preoccupied in other thoughts that the pleasantness of the odor was nonexistent. He followed the scent to its origin.

The kitchen used to be a favorable place to spend time when his mother was still around. Now, it didn't hold the magic it once held. Only his father, a man that he came to despise.

"Don't just stand there, go wash your hands and get ready for dinner." His father was a large man with a hairy chest and arms. He was preparing the table for their meal.

Carl slowly turned and headed for the bathroom. He returned to the kitchen to find his father sitting at the table.

"Hurry, the food is getting cold." After grace was said, they began to eat. The sound of utensils touching chinaware was pronounced. "So son how is church coming along?"

Carl placed his fork on his plate. "The bishop said I'm going to do well under his care."

"Good, whatever the bishop ask of you I want you to adhere to it. Is that understood?"

Carl stared at his father. Doesn't he know what the bishop is asking me to do?

Doesn't he even care?' Carl hated the fact that their features favored. "Yes dad."
They continued eating quietly.

As the meal came to an end, Carl's father stood from the table. "Before you
began the dishes, I want you to bring my drink to the study room."

"Yes sir." It was a habitual request. Every evening his father would drink
himself to sleep. An idea struck in Carl's mind.

Carl brought a fifth of whisky and a clean glass to his father in the study
room. His father sat on the sofa watching the newscaster on the television set. He
sat the items on the table next to his father and departed.

In the kitchen, Carl held his hands in the soapy water of the sink as he
washed the evening dishes. His mind was replaying different scenarios of revenge
against his father. He knew his father was much larger and stronger than himself.
He realized he would have to plan accordingly.

After finishing his chores, Carl quietly entered into the study room. A smile
was produced. As always, his father had drank himself to sleep. Carl headed
down the hallway. He stopped at the closet on the left. The closet space was a
common area where everyone stored different items that wouldn't fit in their own
bedroom closets. He found what he was looking for. His father's golf clubs were
in view. He reached inside the bag and retrieved a number seven driver. That
particular club was used to send the ball a great distance. The steep edge and
sharp siding assured great impact on the ball.

Carl entered the study to find his father fast asleep in his chair. The television
was on. Carl silently approached his father with the club held tightly in his grasp.
He stood in front of his dad as images of his decomposed mother resurfaced in
his mental. He mimicked the sign of the cross with his free hand. He felt a need
to end this chapter in his life. In a smooth motion, Carl drew back the club as if
he was going to hit a ball during a baseball game. He swung the club hard as he

could toward its mark. The metal connected with a dull thud. It was the sound of bone shattering. The impact of the club was precise. The metal connected with his father's throat, directly in the larynx region. Carl could feel the impact on the handle of the club. It felt good to him. Fear-stricken, he watched his father. He witnessed his father's eyes open for a brief moment, then closed. Death had ensued upon impact.

A jolt of the bus hitting rough terrain returned Carl from his reverie. The recollection was a constant reminder for him. He gazed at his watch. He read the location sign. The green and white reflective sign read BLOOMINGDALE. He knew he was only minutes away from Savannah, Georgia.

29

Mount Sinai Hospital was filled with activity on the outside as well as on the inside. Camera crews, reporters, and religious personnel were cordon off from the area. They were located just before the entrance. The police, along with the national guards, worked diligently to keep order and control of the situation. Different religious groups argued the laws concerning the Second Coming.

One particular group was totally against everything that was argued. They felt that their people were being targeted because of their belief system as most middle eastern cultures. Unlike their brethren, they were not dressed in the appropriate religious garbs. They blended in quite nicely with the masses. The only distinguishing trait to tell them apart was a small crescent moon and star tattooed on the right hand, located at the web of the thumb and index digits. They were well-trained for the task at hand. Government officials referred to them as sleeper cells. They were located all around the world working in diverse market places. They were employed in every occupational background imaginable. They stood by awaiting orders to proceed to do what they were trained for. Their unified ideology was to revenge Allah's name and become martyrs doing so. To them it was the highest achievement that could be obtain in human existence. In their cognizance, it would allow them an enriched life in the hereafter.

Hospital security remained heightened. The seventh floor was a high security area. The only admittance into that area was to hospital staff. No visitors of any kind were admitted. Detective Hall could not believe the magnitude of attention the ordeal excited. He was unable to get clearance onto the floor. His federal contact was useless to the situation because the higher-ups believed it to be a national security measure. The snowball effect had begun.

Detective Hall phoned Marlene Sutherland to notify her of the situation.

"Cheer up, there's still a silver lining. The evidence you've sent to me held positive DNA material. I was able to access the database from the codes that you've given me. The hair follicles belong to Carl Brandon. In his file there is a report that speculates he killed his own father. It says his mother was found buried in the backyard of the house. Nothing was ever proved. He was raised in the Catholic diocese afterward."

"Wow! That's good reporting Marlene. That means that the

accusations of him being molested fits the puzzle. Marlene thank you. Are you sure that you don't want to change occupations? You'll make a good detective."

"Forget it! I'm only doing it for you. What's your next move?"

Detective Hall sighed deeply as he contemplated the question. "Since I can't get close to Sister Beatrice, I might as well follow Priest Hamilton. I'm sure he'll lead me to the cash."

"You just be careful. I miss you."

"I miss you too. I'll be back soon." A silence existed on the line. "Thank you Marlene. I have to go now."

"You're welcome." The line was disconnected.

***

The operating room was busy with staff assisting in the labor process of Sister Beatrice. There are thousands of childbearing cases a year in the United States. Because of the status of Sister Beatrice, this one was outstanding. The staff was anxious to see the newborn emerge.

Sister Beatrice was in excruciating agony. She squeezed the pillow tightly.

"Please! Get this baby out of me!"

"Okay, you're doing great. Just breathe deeply," stated the nurse. She was a registered nurse in her mid 30's. She was pleasant and cheerful. She felt privileged to be a part of the team making history as she referred to it.

Another nurse was positioned between her legs watching her dilate. She was concerned about the baby's head and body fitting through the opening. Sister Beatrice's hymen had been surgically cut. A standby team watched the event. A caesarean section was needed to be performed.

"Sister you are doing fine," said the nurse. She dabbed the sweat from Sister Beatrice's brows.

"Ten centimeters!" shouted the nurse positioned between the stirrups.

"Okay, call for the doctor," ordered the head nurse.

***

Dr Saad Al-Mouyad sat in his office reading reports from his computer monitor. He jotted figures on a paper. He was 37 years old. Early signs of balding was prominent. His clean shaven face and rimless eyeglasses gave him a distinctive appearance. Dr Al-Mouyad had been working in that particular hospital for seven years. With the credentials he obtained from his education, he could have went to any of the ivy league hospitals in the country. He was ordered to take the position at that particular location. When he heard about Sister Beatrice coming to his hospital he smiled. After reading the coded message on the screen he felt elated because he waited many years to make his contribution to the cause. Dr Al-Mouyad sat staring at the screen. He used his left hand to rub at the tiny tattoo on his right hand. It was the depiction of a crescent moon and a star. He looked at the tattoo and kissed it.

RING! RING!

He snatched the receiver from the cradle and listened. "Okay, I'll be there." Hanging up the receiver, Dr Al-Mouyad headed toward a locked file cabinet in the corner of the room. Inside the cabinet was a black, leather, belt with a solid square metal buckle. He placed the leather belt on after disregarding the one he adorned. He carefully fastened it around his waist and picked up his stethoscope. He placed it around his neck and headed out of the door.

Dr Saad Al-Mouyad held a pleasant persona as he greeted everyone in his path. He continued walking. He entered an operating room and headed toward the sterilization area.

Adorned in the proper garbs, Dr Al-Mouyad entered into the main chamber to see Sister Beatrice for the first time. He noted that all of the tools needed were laid out on a stainless-steel cart. He was handed a chart with the patient's status.

"Okay, let's see what we have here." He lubricated his latex covered hands and proceeded with assisting with the childbirth process. An hour later, he was able to see the hair covered crown of the newborn.

After the cervix had opened to about four inches, Sister Beatrice was ordered to push with her abdominal muscles in rhythm with the contractions. The action forced the baby through the cervix and out of the vagina. The doctor slowly retrieved the fluid-soaked baby. He cut and clamped the umbilical cord. Covered in amniotic fluid made it hard to tell the baby's characteristics.

Dr Al-Mouyad held the baby up and slapped it gently on the buttocks. Sweat glistened from his brown as a nurse attended to him by dabbing a cloth across his forehead. Dr Saad Al-Mouyad pushed the plate on the buckle of his belt as he held the baby with one hand. The loud shriek emitted from the newborn masked his intentions.

"ALLAH 'AKBAR!" shouted the doctor. The staff looked on perplexed.

At that moment the entire operating room exploded. A bright flash illuminated. The ignition caused a powerful blast from the C4 concentrated in the belt buckle. The force was so powerful, every window in the place shattered from impact. No one survived the blast.

The aftermath left blood, gore, body parts, and medical equipment scattered throughout the disarrayed enclosure. Concrete was everywhere. Smoldering dust, fire, and smoke was omnipresent. It was an unbelievable sight to behold. Security rushed to the scene. The hospital was being evacuated simultaneously. The explosion could be heard outside. On the street side, people rushed frantically for cover. Another terrorist attack on the United Sates is what everyone perceived. The media tried desperately to find answers to the mayhem. They too tried getting an exclusive on the situation. News of the situation went out over the airwaves and around the world.

30

Dr Marlene Sutherland sat at a luncheon table with two of her closest girlfriends. The trio were close-knit. They shared the most intimate moments with one another. Sitting to the left of Marlene was Tracey Campbell. She was a financial journalist and market prognosticator for a business giant. Her husband dreamed of owning his own business but lacked certain personalities. In recent years, she leaped into business by creating a dot-com company. It was a 24 hour telephone and internet service set up to search for business and technical information. It became a huge success. Tracey's hairstyle was in a French braid. Her auburn hair color was natural. She was conscious of her appearance, she always kept in the latest fashion.

Her greenish-blue eyes and creamy skin was radiant.

On the opposite side of her was Dianne Steadford. She was also an entrepreneur. She started making and buying gift items and reselling them to retailers eight years prior. It was at that time she gave birth to Gifts, Hearts, Kisses, and Flowers Inc. The company literally started at the kitchen table in her Atlanta home. Dianne was beautiful. She was bi-racial, her Latin-African American traits were distinguishing. Her caramel complexion was flawless. She had high cheek bone structure. She carried her heritage proudly. Her hair was jet black and lengthy. It hung to the mid point of her back. Her lips were full and her eyes sockets were downturned. She had turned down numerous offers from modeling agencies.

The three ladies sat at a window table. The table was filled with food and drinks. Laughter came with ease because the trio truly adored one another and basked in each other's company.

"Marlene," stated Dianne. "Enough about us. How's your social life? You look to be glowing lately. Are you getting it on the regular?"

All eyes around the table focused toward Marlene. "You heifers are so bad." She smiled. "If you want to know. Yes, I have a prospect. He's a detective in New York City."

"Oh God!" retorted Tracey.

"No, hear me out! He's a really nice guy. Very caring. I've been seeing him off and on."

"How is he in bed? If you don't mind me asking." Dianne placed a spoonful of ice cream into her mouth.

"We haven't gone there yet, but I plan to."

"Just don't get your feelings hurt girl. Being with a cop isn't an easy task. Especially, with waiting up all night and not knowing if he's coming home. That kind of thing can age a woman you know." Tracey's eyes bore into Marlene's.

Dianne's cellphone rang. "Excuse me, I have to take this." She listened to the caller. "Okay, just call her back and confirm. I'm on my way." She disconnected the line. She adverted her attention to her friends. "Duty calls…" She stood and dropped some cash onto the table.

"No, I've got this one. You gold diggers get dinner," said Tracey. The ladies all decided that lunch was officially over.

***

Detective Hall made a call to headquarters. He received information about a United Christian Foundation truck that was reported missing from the area where he now was. He was also informed that the global positioning system onboard the vehicle was still operational.

Armed with pertinent information, Detective Hall arranged for a helicopter to pick him up.

Hovering high over the southern state of Georgia, Detective Hall gazed down at the vast green land. The loud sound of the engine and rotors was discordant. The pilot was preoccupied at the controls. Both men wore helmets with communication equipment attached. It allowed them to speak over the loud din.

"Over there!" shouted the pilot. He pointed toward the east. "That is the Savannah's docking area. It's the largest in the region. It's where the signal is being transmitted from."

The message was received through his headgear with a high-pitched tone and a slight twang. "Okay, see if you can set me down close. I can make if from there."

The whirlybird handled precisely. It landed outside the gated structure of the docking facility. Detective Hall noticed large freighter ships being loaded and unloaded. There were massive amounts of shipping containers everywhere. Trucks and people were moving about inside of the huge complex. It reminded Doug of a city within a citadel. The police helicopter stirred dust around as it departed. Detective Hall covered his eyes until the debris subsided.

He found his way onto the compound using his credentials. Once inside, he began searching for the United Christian Foundation vehicle. The industrial noise inside the Savannah wharf was loud and harsh. The sounds of electromagnetic cranes moved high above, placing huge shipping containers on the ground. The sound vibrated inside his eardrums. An undetectable scent of carbon monoxide from idling tractors awaiting loads was overwhelming. Dock workers were dressed in uniforms and wearing bright orange helmets. They also adorned goggles and ear plugs as they moved about their business of shipping.

Detective Hall moved about purposely. His dark suit, white shirt, and black tie was outstanding amongst the many blue-collar workers. He moved observingly throughout the different sections. There was a giant industrial freightliner with a name at the bow. It was called Sea Goliath. It was moored at the dock and being loaded with containers.

Detective Hall continue onward scanning the vehicles as he passed. *'It has to be here. There are so many damn trucks.'* A dock worker was passing by.

"Excuse me, I would like to ask you a question."

The dock worker, a middle-aged man wearing goggles and a helmet stopped. He looked at the clipboard he held as if in a hurry. "What can I do for ya?"

"I was wondering, if a private customer wanted to ship a container aboard that vessel." He pointed toward the ship. "Where would that take place?"

"If it's private as you say. They would have to scale up over there." The dock worker pointed to another direction.

"Thank you for your help."

"Don't mention it." The dock worker continued onward.

Detective Hall scanned the vehicles in the long convoy. He spotted a vehicle in a long line of other trucks. His heart rate excelled from excitement. He spotted a red and white truck that was labeled United Christian Foundation Incorporation. The logo was that of a red cross with the symbol of a fish. The symbol meant that Jesus was the fisherman of men. He hastened his steps to a near jog as he headed in the direction of the tractor-trailer.

Detective Hall approached the vehicle stealthily. His weapon was drawn. The driver was unaware of what was taking place. Startled, the driver raised his hand in the air at the sight of the semi-automatic, weapon being pointed in his direction. The radio playing in the cab dampened the auditory perception of what the man waving the gun was saying.

"Freeze! Don't move!" shouted the detective forcefully. He saw the driver reaching overhead. Detective Hall braced himself for a confrontation. The driver reached up and turned off the radio.

"Hands where I can see them!" In his peripheral vision, Detective Hall could see that the other drivers were just as surprised as the initial driver. "Open the door and step out of the truck!"

The driver was a man in his 50's. He had salt and pepper colored hair and beard. His hazel green eyes were covered by prescription eyeglasses. He wore denim jeans, sneakers, and tee shirt. The driver stepped out of the vehicle as ordered. "W-what seems to be the problem officer?"

"How many people are with you?"

The driver looked around questionably. "Just me, what is this all about?"

Detective Hall displayed his credentials. "I'm Detective Hall. Place your hand behind your back and face the truck." The driver was handcuffed. He was turned to face Doug.

"What is this all about?"

"What are you hauling?"

"Books, pamphlets, and forms."

"Do you mind if I check the cargo myself?"

The driver looked at him strangely. "If it will clear this up, go right ahead."

"Sit down on your hands," order Detective Hall. He inched toward the trailer. He unfastened the latch and stood to the side. With his weapon pointed, he opened the large panel door. Peering inside the darken cavity, he saw that no one was aboard. 16 pallets of boxes were inside. He climbed aboard and examined the cargo. Satisfied, he disembarked.

"I'm sorry for the inconvenience but we're in a state of emergency. He displayed his identification after and released the driver. "If you have any complaints you can take it up with my boss."

The driver was a devout Christian. He was familiar with the act of forgiveness. "Officer, I know you are a civil servant for the people and only doing your job. I have no discrepancy with you."

"Thank you." Detective Hall felt embarrassed for his ill actions. He began walking away.

"Detective," referred the driver. "If you're looking for someone of this organization, I suggest you try the shipping lanes. That's where they load these babies to go overseas to aid the sick and poor in third world countries."

"Thank you." Detective Hall hurried off toward the shipping area.

***

Detective Hall reached the shipping area. His breathing was heavy from the sprint. A man of Latin descent manned the reception desk.

"May I help you?" asked the clerk. His name plate read Juan Ramirez. The clerk had dark brown skin with hooded eyelids. His air was straight, jet black, and short cropped.

Detective Hall displayed his identification to the clerk. I need to know if any United Christian Foundation trucks have been loaded today."

The clerk looked inside of a ledger book. The title of the book was noticeable. It read LOG-IN MANIFEST. "Yes, there has…" Detective Hall heart rate surged. "but that's not usual. You see there are many missionary services that come through this port daily. As far as UCF, there has been 27 trucks so far."

"I need to inspect all 27 containers."

"That's impossible. The containers are placed strategically throughout the ship. They are positioned according to their arrival. It would be impossible to search through all of them and still allow the ships make its schedule voyage."

"I need to talk to your superior."

A large burly man of Irish descent drove out to the main gate at the request of his clerk. Detective Hall explained the situation to him. He notified to the man about the urgency of the matter.

"I'm sorry, there's nothing I can do without higher orders."

"Okay…" Detective Hall stepped back and retrieved his cellphone. He dialed the federal building in New York. "Director Newhart I'm in Savannah, Georgia. I have reasons to believe that…" He continued to explain his theory of the situation. He also added the dilemma of the shipping dock workers not wanting to comply. Afterward, he listened a few minutes to the response of the director. "Sir are you sure? I can feel this." More listening on Detective Hall's part. "Very well sir." The line was disconnected. Feeling as of he'd been hit with a bag of nickels in the stomach, Detective Hall faced the two men sheepishly. "Okay gentlemen. I'm sorry to have caused you trouble. Excuse me." Detective Hall exited the premises.

Outside in the cool breeze, he headed away from the compound. Just as he cleared the gates, his cellphone rang. He read the caller identification. "Marlene, hi honey. You're definitely a bright spot in the storm."

"You sound exhausted. Are you okay? Have you ate anything today?"

Hearing Marlene's concerned voice made him feel better instantly. She moved his spirit upwards. He explained the snag in the investigation.

"You must not have heard about Sister Beatrice."

"Did she have the baby? What was it? A boy? A girl?" Interjected the detective excitedly.

"Neither, she's dead." Marlene explained the facts of the unfolding news reports.

"Oh my God!" There was a silence on the line.

"Are you still there?" asked Marlene.

"Y-yes, I'm still here. I'm coming home.

31

Carl sat in a dark and cold confinement. The sound of steel slamming against containers was deafening inside the enclosure. Echos magnified tremendously. A loud siren resounded. The containment that Carl was in began to sway. Side to side motioning began to disorient him.

That was the signal he awaited. It was the sign that it was safe to exit from his confinement. A flashlight illuminated the rear part of the compartment. It reassured that he wasn't alone. Another light illuminated, then another. The men inside of the container began to stir and stretch. It was an effort to dissipate stiffness from their joints. Four men headed toward the front of the container. After being loaded at the All Saint Church, the driver waited at the Savannah wharf. When Carl appeared, he was placed in the truck's trailer compartment with three other men. They were needed to make the plan come together. *'I wish I didn't need so many but there's no way around it.'*

Shadowy faces illuminated against the flashlights. One man, taller than all the rest, talked with a slight accent. He wore a cap reversed upon his head. The headgear partially covered his black hair. He had an aquiline nose and beady eyes. His high cheekbone appeared to display a taller appearance. They referred to one another by code names. His name was Wolf. The man next to him in the circle was physically well defined. He was in his mid 30's. He wore a full facial beard that was neatly trimmed. His face was expressionless. The man's stance reflected his military training. He went by the name of Cobra. The man next to him was the same height as Carl. He was much darker in complexion than the others. He appeared to be of middle eastern descent. He went by the code name of Eel.

The Sea Goliath was traveling on the vast Atlantic Ocean. A misty scent of salt waft through the air. Inside the container, where they took up abode, had all the provisions needed to make the long trip. Along with them inside the container were shrink wrapped pallets of boxes. The boxes held red cross markings on them. Inside the cartons were more collected proceeds from the church donations. They were the tithes given faithfully by the flock. There were 18 pallets in all. All 18 pallets contained United States currency of different denominations. Knowing that the United States would never stop coming after him, Carl knew that he had to get out of the country. Finding these mercenaries was easy. Soldiers of Fortune were commonplace. *The plan is coming together. This is just the first part.*

"Everyone, when we get to our destination we will be wealthy men." The men nodded in agreement. One of the soldiers began making the meals for the others to eat. It was a five-day journey to their destination.

"Tell me something," asked Cobra. He sat on the hard, cold, metal floor eating his meal. "What made you think of a scheme so elaborate as this? Did you know it would draw worldwide attention?"

Carl spooned some canned rations into his mouth. He savored the flavor before answering the question. The rest of the men sat around awaiting a response. Carl placed his spoon in the ration can and set it aside. A dull cling sounded from the tin metal hitting against steel as he placed the can on the floor. "You see, I grew up in the church. I've witness enough things behind the scenes to make an unknowing person cringe in disgust. The plan I've put together, I call retribution."

"Do you have any regrets of not being able to step back on United States soil again?" asked Wolf.

"My only regret is that I didn't calculate a faster escape plan with the cash. As you know gentlemen there were well over three of these vehicles to be fill with cash from those religiously starved and ignorant people."

The men gazed toward one another, then continued to eat. When nightfall came around they ventured out on deck to walk and stretch. The nocturnal setting was enchanting; the only illumination stemmed from the moonlit sky and stars. Periodically, other vessel's running lights could be observed passing in the night. The sound of the diesel engine chugging along broke through the natural silence.

Carl stood at the rail of the ship looking over into the twilight darkness. *'I'll be back United States. Believe me, I'll be back.'*

32

Happy to be back, Detective Hall checked in with his superior officers. Afterward he made his way to Marlene's house. He missed her so much; he never had an attraction for anyone as he now felt for Marlene. She had become a bright spot in his life. *'She's smart, beautiful, and pleasant to be around. I hit the Jackpot!'* He was happy to have more to think about than work. Sister Beatrice appeared in his cognizance. *'She didn't deserve to die that way.'* Anger swelled up in his being at the thought. His mind was on Carl Brandon. *'I'll get you, that you can count on!'*

 After stopping at his apartment to change clothes, Detective Hall found his way to Marlene's apartment. Prior to arriving, he visited a famous chocolatier in the area. The establishment dealt in candies imported from all over the globe. The delightful aroma of fine sweets and wafers waft through the air. It was hypnotic to his senses. Detective Hall rang the doorbell.

Marlene answered the door wearing a light and airy sundress. The material had a paisley designs. Her hair was fixed in Jersey curls. Her face was done lightly with makeup. Hoop earrings accentuated her outfit. Exquisite was the one word that described her beauty.

"Come in." Marlene's smile exposed perfect teeth. She stepped aside allowing Doug entrance into her home. She was delighted to see he was dressed in causal clothing. He wore designer slacks, a button up shirt under a mock neck sweater. A pair of leather, loafers accentuated the ensemble. Marlene noticed he carried a small shopping bag. "What's in the bag?"

Detective Doug Hall couldn't help from staring at her natural beauty. His eyes gazed at the bag that he carried. "Oh, I thought that maybe we could stay here. I've brought you something to add to your essence." He handed her the box containing chocolates. "Sweetness."

Marlene blushed as she received the box. "Thank you. Have a seat and make yourself comfortable while I fix us something to eat."

"Better yet, why don't I help you? You'll be surprised at what I can do in the kitchen."

"That's a deal." They headed into the kitchen.

Ninety minutes later, they were sitting down to an appealing meal. The meal consisted of lemony tortellini with peas and prosciutto. The meal was stunningly prepared by Doug. Marlene fixed the salad. It was a rhubarb and kale confetti salad. The use of multi-color vegetables gave the salad an appealing sensation. Together the meal went well. The two felt as if they were in an Italian restaurant. The best part was they had the comfort of home.

Marlene enjoyed the meal and Doug's company. *'Wow! This is too good to be true.'* His smile was inward. "Where did you learn to prepare a dish like this?"

Doug dabbed his lips with a napkin. "My mother was a teacher and an opportunist. She instilled in me to learn as much as I could. So cooking became one of my curriculums. Now it's your turn. You are a great doctor, why not have your own private practice? You're more than qualified."

Marlene took a sip of white wine. "I've thought about it. I've also thought about changing courses in my career. I was thinking about becoming a pediatrician. I love children."

"Okay, I'm stuffed. How about you?" asked Doug. Marlene nodded in agreement. "What do you say we watch a movie?"

"Sounds great. You go ahead and make some drinks while I clear the table. I'll join you afterwards."

Doug and Marlene cuddled around the fireplace watching the latest movie. Marlene felt so relaxed and secure in the presence of Doug. Everything felt right. To his belief, being with Marlene was fate. It was a destiny that was being fulfilled. Seemingly, he could feel Marlene's pulse align with his own. Their eyes met. It was as if each one could understand the other's needs. Their lips met. It had been some time for Marlene to have been sexually active with anyone. She was ripe for the encounter.

"Take me Doug."

Doug carried Marlene into the bedroom. Gently, he placed her on a satin covered queen-size bed. The decor and color scheme was creme and lavender. Scented candles filled the air with a pleasant aroma of lilac.

Doug began to slowly undress her. As the layers of garments were removed, Doug's heart rate excelled from excitement. Witnessing her flawless beauty was pleasurable. *'I've never saw anyone so beautiful.'* Marlene stared into his eyes as her breathing became excited from passion. She lie on the bed wearing nothing but a designer silk and lace undergarments.

Doug stood back from the bed to take in the view. He began undressing himself in a burlesque manner. As he remove his shirt and tee shirt, he could see how Marlene's eyes marveled at his defined sculpted body. After removing his trousers, he neared the bed.

Marlene began to feel his body. The sensual sensation of her hand moving across the ripples of muscles turned her on completely. Doug began unfastening her bra to release her D-cup breasts from captivity. Her cocoa complexion and slightly darker areoles displayed perfection. Her nipples stood erect awaiting attention from him. Doug wasted no time. He kissed her sensual, puffy lips. He continued south. Marlene's perfume drove him wild. His moistened tongue began gently licking and sucking at her breast and nipples.

Marlene pleasurably moaned. Her senses were heightened tremendously. He continued down further but Marlene stopped him. Without explanation, she pushed him on his back and began caressing his body while kissing his chest. She could feel his hardness press against her thigh. She continued further as she felt his manhood. Marlene placed her hands into his shorts and uncovered his love shaft. Impressed with its dimension, she began to stroke his member. Placing his shaft into her moisten mouth, she sucked fervently. Slurping noise existed. Doug could feel the back of her tonsils as she deep throated his member. She discontinued her actions, relieving him of his undershorts. As Doug lie back facing upward, she mounted him. His stiff shaft entered into her eagerly awaiting love canal.

"Yes, that's it…" Marlene was in a frenzy. The sensation of pure pleasure envelope her as she bounced up and down on his blood engorged penis. She concentrated on her vaginal muscles and squeezed them around his shaft.

Doug felt the tightening sensation around his member. The sensation was mixed with a warm silkiness from her wet vagina. The feeling was blissful. He could feel the charge of electromagnetic attraction making him want to climax. He fought hard to avoid eruption. Changing position, he took control by positioning her on her back. He placed her legs on both shoulders. The position gave him access to deep penetration. He entered her warm, wet canal. Their eyes locked as he deeply stroked her gently. As the moments passed, so did the tempo. They moved synchronously until they were drenched in perspiration.

"I can't hold out any longer! I'm cum…." His thrust became more intense. He pounded uncontrollably harder and more sporadic.

"Don't stop!" Marlene was caught in a frenzy. "Fuck me! Harder! Harder!"

The two cuddled in bed staring up at the ceiling. Their breathing was heavy.

"I want you to know this wasn't a fling. I really want to be with you."

Marlene studied his demeanor. "You don't have to explain anything. I feel the same way. Let's take it a moment at a time." Marlene raised from the bed. "I'm going to take a shower." She winked slyly. "If you want more meet me there." She headed out of the room naked.

Doug was left feeling satisfied and content. Being with Marlene was complete bliss. She is who he wanted. She was who he needed.

33

The Sea Goliath docked in Spain. They were located at a seaport near the Strait of Gibraltar. The port was located in an industrial town called Faro. It was a seaport that was on the connecting side of Spain. It was the location where the Mediterranean Ocean and the Atlantic Ocean divided Spain and North Africa.

Carl and the group exited the cargo ship and made arrangements for transportation for when their container was unloaded. Carl saw that the majority of the people were of color. They worked diligently at the dock. The salty air and the sea mist was more pertinent than out at sea.

A truck commanded by the crew took their container to a house on a mountainous hilltop. The house was a wooden structure that was in desperate need of maintenance. What made the place so ideal was that it was secluded from any neighboring town. From its high elevated position any intruder approaching could be detected a mile before it actually arrived. Even from aerial support.

The men settled in. Afterward, their hefty fee was paid. In the rear of the house was four smaller trucks parked under sheds. The men placed their possessions into separate vehicles. Simultaneously, they headed down the hillside, leaving Carl alone in the house.

Carl waited outside in front of the house watching the three vehicles depart. The trucks kicked up dirt in their wake. In efforts to not waste any valuable time, Carl boarded a truck and headed back down the hillside in the direction in which he came.

He approached a bridge that separated Spain from North Africa. Carl crossed over after clearing customs. *'Strange what money can buy here.'* He continued his drive into Morocco toward a capital city called Rabat. The location held a large population of more than 20 million people. The city had an archaic appearance. Its cultural heritage stood out in the center square. The neighboring areas were modern with high-rise buildings and neon lights as the big cities abroad. His first stop was a private Moroccan bank. It was through referral that he knew of its existence.

Carl and the executive branch director sat across from one another in his office. It was a towering building. They were on the 27th floor. The director was of African descent. His complexion was dark. His hair was curly. His facial features were distinguished. His wide nose told of his African tribal ancestry of the Bantu people. He wore a dark suit that was the color of cream. He also wore a white, starched shirt and a silk tie. A small ring was on his finger. He wore a designer watch on his wrist. His name was Naim Dbween.

"As you know we have the most discreet clients in the world. Your money will be safe. Our rates you will find them most appealing."

Carl was satisfied. "Deal! Where do I sign?"

***

Carl entered into a private clinic that was referred to him by the same people that suggested the private bank in Morocco. Surprisingly, it was located in a seedy part of the city. Inside, the interior took on a better view. It was nicely decorated and quaint. A reception desk came into view as he entered. Sitting at a station was a middle-aged Moroccan woman. She had a sandy brown complexion with dark circles around her eyes. Her liquid brown eyes bore into Carl's.

"Yes? May I help you?" Her accent was pronounced.

"I have an appointment with Dr Raja Sedeka. My name is Carl Winston."

Quickly, she began typing with the used of her keyboard while studying the screen. Carl looked around the office to see that the place seemed deserted. The receptionist adverted her eyes up toward Carl. "Yes, I see it. The doctor will see you, but first you must be prepped. She pressed a button under the desk. Shortly after, a young beautiful nurse entered the reception area. Her complexion was caramel. Her figure was full. She displayed flawless, smooth skin. The nurse wore a white smock atop her personal clothing. A name tag was attached to her breast pocket. It read M Tsug. Her silky, jet black, hair was fixed in a French braid.

"Mr Winston, please follow me."

The receptionist nodded to Carl as a gesture of approval. He was led through a stainless-steel door.

Inside, the nurse led him to a seat in an examining room. A man in a white smock and black slacks was studying some documents at his desk. The doctor stopped what he was doing and stood to greet Carl.

"Glad that you made it. Everything is all set."

Carl reached into his jacket pocket and produced an overstuffed envelope. He handed it to the doctor. "Just as we agreed upon."

"Mr Winston will you please take off your jacket, shirt, and put on this garment…" The nurse handed him a lime green smock. Carl began doing what was asked. "Will you please lie upon the table." The stainless steel table held a comfortable cushion. Carl was positioned faced up. An adjustable light was placed above his head. A bright aqua blue light blanketed his entire face.

"Mr Winston I am just going to take an outline measurement of the related area. Please try to relax." The doctor began making a series of lines with a special marker. The device was a digital and wireless stylus. The instrument graphically recorded the data of strokes made by the marker. When the information was programmed into the computer, the user would be able to adjust any measurements desired. A computer image with the patient's facial data would be downloaded into the program. This allowed the doctor to see a metamorphosis of the work intended before the actual procedure took place.

The nurse busied herself with the preparations of the tools that were to be used for the procedure. Steam emitted from a sterilization machine in the far corner of the room. The nurse extracted tools from the machine using thick rubber gloves. She placed the steaming hot metal tools on a sterilized mobile cart. She wheeled it over to the table next to Mr Winston.

"Mr Winston I am going to administer to you a sedative that will render you unconscious. Please, just relax."

After being placed under sedation, the nurse and doctor went about the business of cosmetic surgery. The entire six hour procedure consisted of removing live tissue and replacing it with a synthetic gel. It was a painstaking process for both the doctor and nurse. That was one of the reasons for the high fees that were charged. The work was quality. The most encouraging fact was that discretion was a priority. No authentic personal data was ever used.

34

Detective Hall sat in a conference room. He was positioned next to Director Newhart. The meeting was set up with only short notice. Doug arrived at the federal building feeling ill willed. He remember feeling abandoned when he tried to get permission to have the Sea Goliath searched for the United Christian Foundation vehicles. *'I was very close.'*

"I know that you are probably still upset at the fact that I didn't back you up on the Savannah wharf deal, but there was reasons." Doug eyed the director suspiciously. "We've been on this case from the very beginning. We have men positioned throughout the area on top of this case. After the incident with Sister Beatrice, we knew that Dr Mouyad was a sleeper cell. This thing is probably bigger than you or I can imagine. That's why I didn't approve your request. If you were right and intercepted their movement at that time. We didn't know what the ramifications it could have caused. We didn't feel prepared to jeopardize the general public."

"So what do we do now?" asked Detective Doug Hall. He was intrigued at the turn of the conversation.

"Okay, I'm not suppose to disclose this. The United Christian Foundation truck is within our radar. You were right, that truck was nearby. We've tracked it to Spain. We have teams in the area as we speak. I will keep you informed on the turn of events because you have done an excellent job from the very beginning."

***

The United Christian Foundation of Macon, Georgia was located in Monroe County. Sitting on four acres were trucks, warehouse docking and equipment. A large ranch style office was also erected.

Inside, workers were manning telephones. Some were doing clerical duties. Numerous file cabinets filled the area. Detective Hall had made an appointment to visit that chapter of the foundation after talking with Director Newhart. Doug had an inkling about the entire situation. *'Something doesn't gel here.'*

Detective Hall sat in a nicely decorated office across from an attractive woman of African-American descent. She was sitting at her desk. Periodically, her eyes studied the computer monitor as she spoke with Detective Hall. Her beautiful features were most pleasant to his eyes. Her smile was captivating. Detective Hall was mesmerized by her golden brown complexion and almond shaped eye sockets.

"…is there any data on the truck that went missing?" asked Detective Hall.

The foundation director, Miss Grainger, began tapping on her keyboard. The sound of her highly glossed fingernails made clacking noise as her fingers quickly passed over the keys. "Here we go. Yes, three days ago today. The driver reported it missing as he reported to work. You see, the driver parked the vehicle and left. He returned the next day for a repeated performance. That's when he noticed the truck missing." She faced Doug. Her brown eyes gleamed at him. "He thought that the truck was pulled out of the fleet for repairs."

"May I have the driver's name and address?"

"Why? Do you think that something underhanded is going on within the foundation?"

"No, it's just a routine check covering all the bases. That's all." She wrote down the information requested and handed it to Doug.

"Thank you."

***

In a small town in Douglass County, Detective Hall knocked on a wooden door. The porch that he stood upon creaked as he shifted his weight. He noticed that the entire structure was in need of

172

maintenance. No one came to the door. He peered into the house through a window adjacent to the porch. The curtains were drawn back. The house was deserted as far as Doug could tell. The interior was just as bad as the exterior. The furniture looked to be from many years ago. It was worn and dusty. Paint peeled from the walls in the living room. *'Okay, money could be a motive here.'* Suddenly, Detective Hall heard a hammering sound resonating from the rear of the house. He headed in that direction as he kept his hand on his concealed holstered weapon.

The sound of metal on metal being hammered crescendoed as Doug approached. He noticed that the sound came from a person underneath a 1975 Monte Carlo. The vehicle had seen better days. Rust and corrosion infected the exterior. Only half of the man's body was exposed as he was positioned on the grassy ground. The display of worn boots and jeans were exposed. The front two wheels of the vehicle were propped on two wooden blocks. The sound was maximally intensified as Detective Hall stood over the man. The man was still hammering away. The harsh sound ceased momentarily.

"Excuse me Mr Walton. May I have a moment of your time?" asked Doug. He stood over the half figure.

Using a mechanic creeper, the man slid from under the vehicle. His face was marred with black grease. His hands were also soiled. Age lines outlined his facial features. At first thought, Doug noticed his eyes. They were dark and liquid. His eyelids drooped over the sockets, giving him a sleepy appearance. Gray hair upon his head contrasted the with the black grease on his face.

"Hand me that rag." The man's voice was deep baritone. He spoke clear and concise. Doug done as asked. He watched the man wipe the grease from his hands.

"How do you know my name?"

"I'm Detective Hall." He displayed his identification to the man. "I'm investigating the disappearance of the truck that was stolen from the foundation."

"It says here…" The old man pointed to the identification. "That you are from New York City. That's a long ways from 'round here."

"The implications has complicate connections."

"Oh I see. What do you want to know?"

"Well…" Doug stooped to the man's eye level as he continued to sit on the ground. "Did anyone ever approach you prior to the vehicle coming up missing? Did anything strange happen out of the ordinary?"

Mr Walton continued wiping his hands on the soil cloth. "Nothing I can remember off hand. You see, I used to run freight for 37 years. Then medical issues with my wife caused me into early retirement in order to tend to her needs."

"Is she home? Maybe I…"

"She died."

"I am so sorry. I didn't know."

Mr Walton held up a hand defiantly. "I began volunteering my time to the foundation to take away the loneliness." Doug could see that he was telling the truth. Emotional pain poured out as he spoke. "No, I can't think of anyone that would steal from an organization that is helping people all over the world."

"Okay, thank you for your time Mr Walton." Detective Hall headed toward his vehicle feeling frustrated at the turn of events.

FIVE

MONTHS

LATER

35

Detective Hall sat in his office during the midday. He eyed a fixture on his desk. It was metal balls held in formation by strings. The formation was a tight, straight line. The apparatus was designed to be scientific and therapeutic. He drew back one of the steel balls at one end of the line and released it. The physics of the gadget allowed him to see how energy had the power to pass through objects to effect its intended target. The released ball hammered into the next one in line, causing a chain reaction. The eyes were only able to detect the last ball in the formation to move. As that ball returned from its pendulum swing, it also passed its energy in the opposite direction through the body of the middle balls effecting the primary ball. Sharp clatter from the apparatus resounded in the quiet office.

His mind was on the fruitless months of investigative research for Priest Hamilton. He noticed the federal authorities began declining to share information with him. Their claim was the case had become a national security issue that he was not cleared for. Doug picked up the telephone and dialed.

***

Dr Marlene Sutherland picked up the receiver on her desk. She was just going over some scheduled surgery reports when the telephone ran.

"Hello? Dr Sutherland speaking. Hey baby, what's going on?"

"I was just thinking about you and decided to give you a call."

Marlene produced a smile. She picked up on his tone. "Tell me what's really going on, and don't say it's nothing."

It was Doug's turn to smile. The fact that she could pick up on his demeanor pleased him. Through the months of courting, the two became close. There was no secrets between them. "I'm just feeling a need for change, that's all."

"Would you like to talk about it over lunch? My treat?"

Doug chortled. "Sounds enticing, but I'll have to pass. I have reports that are way overdue. How about I meet you at your apartment tonight and we can discuss it?"

"Okay."

Doug replaced the receiver on the cradle. He felt good after hearing Marlene's voice. She became a staple in his diet for happiness.

***

"You what?" asked Marlene.

"I feel like quitting. I don't want to play cops no more. What's the big deal? I hope you didn't fall in love with me for my uniform." It was said in a jokingly manner.

Marlene smiled. "You don't wear a uniform. You are a detective that wear suits." Laughter ensued. They sat next to one another on a sofa in the living room.

"Seriously, I've been doing a lot of thinking about it. I was thinking maybe you and I can get out of this godforsaken rat race and live. We both are still young, we've saved enough money to live comfortable." He sighed deeply. Doug moved from the couch to one knee in front of Marlene. He produced a black velvet box that contained an engagement ring he'd purchased months ago but didn't have the courage to give it to her. Today he felt different. Everything felt so right. Doug could feel a new chapter in his life about to began.

Doug opened the box displaying a beautiful diamond ring. The ring sat on an elegantly sculptured, platinum table. The stone bedazzled with shimmering light of iridescence.

Marlene was truly amazed and surprised. The act was unanticipated. The unguarded moment was shockingly astonishing for her.

Doug looked directly into her brown eyes. "I was thinking maybe you wouldn't mind becoming Mrs Hall. Will you please except this token as a symbol of my love for you?"

Tears of endearment flowed down her cheeks. "Yes, I would love to become your wife." She held out her hand for Doug to consummate the event by placing the ring on her finger. The symbolic gesture was sealed with a passionate kiss.

***

Marlene sat at a luncheon table with her best friends. Seated at the table was Tracey Campbell. She was wearing a light and airy sundress. Her hair was done in a French braid style. Seated across from her was Dianne Steadford. She was wearing a cream colored pair of slacks and an olive colored blouse.

"Who called this meeting so abruptly?" asked Tracey. "Did someone die?"

"I called this meeting. And no, no one died. In fact, just the opposite," confessed Marlene.

"Well it better be good because I was shopping for a new car."

"What's wrong with your car? You just purchased it a few months back," retorted Dianne. She picked up her glass and sipped.

"Well for starters, that's just the privileges of success."

"I called you ladies here because you are my best friends."

"Girl what's gotten into you? You look like you fell into a bed and woke up with roses," interjected Tracey. She chewed on a pastry.

"Close, it's not what's gotten into me. It's who's gotten into me. Only thing is I came up sparkling." Marlene outstretched her hand to allow her ring to bedazzle the group.

Both ladies were caught off guard. Tracey and Dianne held their hands in front of their mouths as is to stifle screams. Excitement ruled the moment. Everyone was excited for Marlene.

"You little hooker. How did you pull that off?" asked Tracey.

"Doug proposed to me yesterday at my apartment." Marlene's smile was broad.

Both women examined the ring simultaneously. They displayed pure delight for Marlene. Dianne stopped a passing waiter.

"Can we have a bottle of champagne?" Dianne adverted her attention back to the girls. "It's time for a celebration. Have you guys set a date as of yet? asked Dianne.

"No! Please, one step at a time."

"You are glowing girl," stated Tracey. She was obviously amused.

Marlene was also excited. "I feel awesome. Doug makes me feel like a school girl with a crush on her teacher. He really makes me feel needed. I feel really secure in this relationship."

"Good, good. You deserve it child."

The champagne arrive and the ladies made a toast to the occasion.

"This is for continued happiness for us three through the years to come. No matter how heavy the wind and rain pours down upon us, may we endure and continue in the union of friendship. I love you guys," said Tracey. The clinging sound of glasses touching resonated in the restaurant.

ONE

YEAR

LATER

36

JOHN F. KENNEDY INTERNATIONAL AIRPORT
ARRIVAL GATE/ C
QUEENS, NEW YORK
1:33 PM

Ralph Sabian exited the aircraft and headed down a ramp. He was met by a swarm of commuters moving about. A discordant murmur lingered in the building. It was the accumulation of talking from the patrons.

'Good old New York City.' He hailed a taxicab and ordered the driver to take him to an address in Brooklyn. During the ride he recollected on different scenarios. In Morocco, during the healing process after his cosmetic surgery, Carl kept up with the current events in the states. He read every article he could get his hands on about the mishaps concerning the All Saint Church. One particular article captured his interest concerning the case. It was about a New York

City detective that was going above and beyond the call of duty to locate the culprits responsible. Other articles recalled how the detective's extensive research showed the priest was responsible for multiple murders before his disappearance. He also read the detective was quoted never to give up until the case was closed. After getting the cosmetic facial reconstruction, Carl had his identification documents altered also. He was now Ralph Sabian, a private investor. He returned to the states with a new agenda. His mission was to quiet Detective Hall. He wanted to stay in North Africa and Spain but for what he craved to do the population there was too small. 90 percent of the people practiced the Muslim faith.

The taxicab stopped in front of a car rental station. 30 minutes later, Ralph Sabian drove from the rental lot with a mid-size vehicle. His reason for choosing that particular vehicle was it was commonplace and compact. Also, it blended in quite nicely with the scheme of things. He didn't want to draw attention to himself.

Using a photograph of Detective Hall he discovered in the newspaper, Ralph Sabian headed toward the detective's place of business. As he drove toward his destination, he viewed himself using the rearview mirror. The action brought about a smile because he wasn't used to the image of the man in the mirror. *'That doctor sure was good. Worth every penny.'* He marveled at his new facial features. His nose was now shorter and slender. There was no more dark circles under his eyes. His lips took on a new definition. *'That's right Ralph, you are no longer that Carl Hamilton guy.'* He found merriment in the thought.

Ralph came to a stop in the East New York section of Brooklyn.

He parked the vehicle across from the 71st Precinct and waited in the car.

***

After receiving an anonymous tip from a caller, Detective Hall raced from the precinct into his unmarked sedan. The color of the vehicle blended in with other commuters. Dark cumulus clouds hovered above in the overcast sky. His tires screeched as he accelerated down the street.

Ralph spotted him. He began to follow at a safe distance. *'Once I take care of you, I can get my church up and running again.'*

Doug pulled to a curb in a seedy section of the city. He exited the vehicle and raced through a debris laden vacant lot. A cutout in the fence gave him direct access. He treaded over broken glass, trash, and drug paraphernalia. A distinctive crunching sound ensued as his boot trampled upon the littered ground. On the grounds, next to an old abandoned vehicle, was a decomposed body. *'I'll be damn, it's just as the caller said.'* Although the body was decaying, Detective Hall was able to identify the body belonging to the murderer who he was searching for in the killing of a woman. The suspect had murdered the woman in front of her young daughter. Detective Hall had been on the hunt for the deceased, low-life for quite some time. A malodorous stench emitted from the corpse. Detective Hall stooped near the body. Using a fountain pen, he inspected a bulge under the perpetrator's jacket. Moving the material back, he saw it was a flashlight in the pocket. *'Hmm, I wonder what you were up to?'* Detective Hall stood and retrieved his two-way radio. He began notifying the dispatcher of the situation.

Within minutes, official vehicles converged on the scene with their emergency lights illuminated. After explaining to his constituents about the incident leading to the find, Detective Hall headed toward his vehicle. He'd seen enough.

Ralph Sabian watched the commotion from a safe distance. *'Hmm, I wonder what's that all about? Nonetheless, I've got you on my radar Mr Detective.'* A slight chuckle ensued. He watched Detective Hall enter his vehicle, then drive away. Ralph placed his vehicle in gear and continued his pursuit of Detective Hall at a safe distance. *'I wonder what he would think if he knew the hunter was being hunted?'*

37

Marlene had a nice dinner awaiting for Doug when he arrived. She felt an inkling that something wasn't right. She noticed that he seemed preoccupied in thought. They sat around the dinner table without conversation. It was something out of the norm for them. The only sound that existed was the noise from the fine chinaware and silverware.

"What's the matter? And don't tell me nothing is bothering you." She placed her fork down and dabbed at the corner of her lips with a napkin.

Doug was suddenly returned from his reverie. He stared into her beautiful eyes. "Noth…" He hesitated as he refrained from answering with an unthoughtful phrase. "I guess it's just work-related stress."

"Then amuse me with it."

Doug placed his utensil on the table. He sighed slightly. "I finally caught up with the guy responsible for turning a little girl into an orphan a few years back."

"So why the gloom? I would think it would have brought you joy."

"He was dead when I arrived at the scene. I'd gotten an anonymous tip. That's the part that have me pickled. Who would do that? And why call it in after he's dead? No, I think there's more to it than that."

"Maybe you're right. I say just keep an open-mind when you're going about your business."

"You're right." Doug sighed deeply. "Babe, I have an early engagement with the upper brass in the morning. Do you mind if we continue this tomorrow?"

Marlene sensed the situation bothered him greatly. She decided not to push it any further. "No, that will be fine. I'll walk you downstairs."

Ralph Sabian watched from a safe distance in the confines of his vehicle. His attention was on Detective Hall. He watched as he embraced and kissed an attractive woman in front of an apartment building. *'Hmm, pretty lady. This may change things.'* He continued observing as Detective Hall parted company with the woman. He watched as the detective entered his vehicle. He drove off leaving the woman behind as she waved. An idea struck Carl. He remained in the vehicle out of sight.

***

6:15 AM

Marlene exited her house. She was dressed for work. She entered her vehicle and began heading for work. At the hospital, she headed for her office. She checked her schedule for the day and began doing her daily duties.

8:30 PM

Marlene exited her vehicle and headed home. She was tired and exhausted. The day's work was overwhelming. All she could think of was a warm bath and relaxation. *'If Doug comes over I'll order take-out. I'm too exhausted to cook.'*

During his visit to the hospital, Ralph did extensive intel on Dr Sutherland. Satisfied with the results, he waited in his vehicle. He was located in the staff parking area. He spotted Dr Sutherland returning from work. She was heading toward her vehicle. Keeping a safe distance, he followed her. She entered her apartment. A few minutes after she entered, a light at a second floor window illuminated. Ralph smiled as another thought occurred. He started the engine in the vehicle. He drove off blending in with the evening traffic.

38

FEDERAL BUREAU OF INVESTIGATION
FRAUD DIVISION/8TH FLOOR
ONE FEDERAL PLAZA
MANHATTAN, NEW YORK

Detective Hall sat inside the office of Assistant Director Greg Porter. The detective sat opposite Mr Porter. They were separated by a polished cherrywood desk.

"I called you here today to give you a heads up on that Carl Hamilton guy. Our trail went cold. It seems we followed him into Morocco and he gave us the slip somehow."

Detective Hall stared across the desk at Mr Porter in disbelief. "What are you saying?"

We believe that he might try to reenter the country. We have a lookout for him. Meanwhile, I would like for you to keep your eyes open."

Detective Hall stood abruptly. He was frustrated. "I don't believe you guys. I almost had the bastard in Savanna but no, you guys wouldn't assist me. Now what are you going to do? Or is that information also above my clearance level?" He used his hands to make air quotations to emphasize the question.

"Please detective take a seat, there's more."

Detective Hall eyed the director with interest as he sat. "Okay, I'm all ears."

"Well…" The director shuffled some papers on his desk. "Intel informs us that a doctor is in custody in Morocco. He is one of he best plastic surgeon on the black market in Northern Africa."

"What does that have to do with anything?"

"We have reason to believe our priest used his services, which means we have no idea of what he may look like now. Hell, he could be in this building at this very moment and we wouldn't know."

Detective Hall rubbed his forehead as frustration mounted. I can't believe it." He stood again, only this time he headed for the door. He exited the premises unescorted.

Outside, he studied the faces of passersby. He tried to configure which one could resemble the priest. *This is insane!* He headed toward his vehicle. His mind continued to plague him with unsettling thoughts.

***

Dr Marlene Sutherland sat behind her desk catching up on

paperwork. A knock came to the door. She approached and opened the door slowly. It was her secretary. The woman was tall and sleek with plain features. Being a middle-aged woman, her physical features were outstanding. She wore her hair in a French braid. She adorned a light blue, conservative, skirt suit.

"Dr Sutherland, there's a Ralph Sabian here to see you. He says it's urgent."

Dr Sutherland studied her secretary for a moment. She sighed deeply. "Okay, you can show him in." Marlene's mind wandered.

The stranger dressed in a black, two-piece suit entered into Dr Sutherland's office space. Dr Sutherland stood to greet the well-groomed stranger.

"Hi, I'm Dr Sutherland. What can I do for you?" Marlene extended out her hand.

"I am sorry to impose on you unannounced. My name is Detective Sabian." They shook hands. "I'm in the same division with Detective Hall." He produced his fraudulent credentials.

Hearing Doug's name caused concern for Marlene. "W-what is it? Is something wrong?" Marlene's heartbeat raced. Pure adrenaline entered her bloodstream. She braced herself for the news.

"There's been a mishap but not to worry, he's not injured. He requested for you to come. That is the extent of what I can explain to you at this time. Will you come with me please?"

"Oh my God! Sure…" Marlene's mind was in overdrive. She tried to focus on what was happening. She began to think the worse case scenarios. She was extremely worried. All she could imagine was Doug being held up somewhere calling for her. She grabbed her jacket off the rack along with her purse and followed.

On the street, they hurried toward his vehicle. Marlene was so worried about Doug she didn't give much thought to the fact the detective drove a black, cargo van instead of a standard sedan. She entered.

"Please, fasten your seat belt."

Ralph wasted no time. He started the engine. He reached into the console and removed a linen scarf. He quickly placed the material over Dr Sutherland nose and mouth, forcing her to breathe the chemical laced scarf.

Marlene struggled. Her seat belt restricted her movement. Within seconds, she remained docile. She sat there disoriented. She succumbed to darkness. The sweet taste and pleasant aroma of chloroform had its effect. He placed a pair of dark sunglasses over her eyes. To the onlookers, Dr Sutherland appeared vibrant.

'Okay sweetie, it's almost finished. Soon I'll have other followers. This time I'll show them the way to the true God.'

The black, cargo van stopped in front of an old run-down house in a seedy section of Far Rockaway, Queens. The house was just off of Beach Channel Drive. Ralph rifled through Dr Sutherland's purse. He searched for a specific item. Leaving the purse inside the vehicle, he carried Dr Sutherland's limp body into the house. The block was quiet. There were only three dwellings on the block. Most of the properties were vacant lots and abandoned buildings. The streets were littered and the grass everywhere was overgrown.

Dr Sutherland was placed on a dusty, queen-size bed. She was restrained with the use of plastic zip ties on her hands and feet. Ralph went into the living room to began the next part of his plan.

Using the cellphone that he had taken from Dr Sutherland's purse, Ralph scanned the menu looking for Detective Hall's telephone number. He found it quickly and speed dialed.

39

Detective Hall drove aimlessly on the Franklin D Roosevelt Drive in his unmarked sedan. He was cognitively trying to get a handle on the situation with the dead body and the priest. He looked over at the directional sign that read 33rd Street. *'I'm already in Midtown. I may as well treat myself to lunch.'*

Detective Hall sat at a window seat enjoying his delicious lunch. The meal consisted of a T-bone steak smothered in onions, a hot baked potato, garlic bread, and salad. He chased the lunch down with a cold glass of beer. Usually, Doug didn't drink during duty but he felt he needed something to take the edge off of all that has happened. Doug's cellphone rang just as he filled his mouth with salad. Quickly, he swallowed beer to wash down the salad. He studied the name and number on the screen. Marlene's name and number was displayed. The sight of her name on the screen cause him to smile and feel secure within. He answered the call.

"Hello? Marlene…" From that moment thereafter, Doug listened to the strange voice on his cellphone. He knew it was dialed from Marlene's cellphone. "What do you want?"

***

Regardless of what the caller stated about coming alone, Doug felt the need for backup. He dialed the station. He informed his captain about the situation. An interceptor was linked to his cellphone in the case the caller dialed his number again.

As he drove in his vehicle, Doug called the hospital where Marlene worked. The receptionist informed him of her rushing out of the door with a detective after he said her presence was requested.

'Oh my, if anything happens to her.' Doug tried to push the negative thought far from his mind. *'Think Doug, think!'* The vehicle came to a full stop at a red light. Frustrated, he banged on the dashboard. Impatiently, he turned on the siren in effort clear a path to pass. He used Flatbush Avenue roadway until he came in contact with the Marine Parkway Bridge. He chose that route figuring if a trap existed maybe he would see it coming. *'I wonder how many are in on this scheme?'* There were so many unanswered variables. Frustration mounted within.

The vehicle continued racing at high speeds through the street.

Detective Hall picked up his radio microphone and keyed it.

"This is Zero-Two-Eight. Do we have eyes in the sky yet?" Static erupted between transmissions.

"Roger Zero-Two-Eight..." High pitched squelch invaded the interior of the vehicle. "ETA is five minutes."

"Roger out!"

He continued onward. Images of Marlene being captured by unknown perpetrators made it harder for Detective Hall to cope. It was now a personal vendetta. *'Please, if you're out there, I'm asking for a favor. Please return her to me.'*

***

Ralph Sabian entered the cargo van. He drove three quarters of a mile to an elevated train station. He parked the vehicle and boarded an A-train.

The A-train traveled two stops along Beach Channel Drive. Mott Avenue was the end of the line for that train. Ralph exited the train with other commuters. The streets were busy with pedestrian traffic. He headed eastbound. He stopped in front of a McDonald's restaurant. He entered and took a seat near a window. The position allowed him the visibility to view his surroundings and whoever entered the restaurant. Ralph sat with a vanilla milkshake and a large order of french fries in front of him. He checked his watch and waited. He kept a keen lookout for Detective Hall. He knew that he had the advantage because he knew what Detective Hall looked like. For him it was the ultimate surprise because no one knew his identity. He gazed at his watch as he sipped on his vanilla milkshake. His mind was in motion of the next step to his plan.

Detective Hall was nearing the rendezvous. He turned on his two-way radio and keyed the microphone. "Okay people, I'm almost there. Make sure there's no uniforms in the area."

"Roger that detective," responded the dispatcher. High pitch static erupted with the transmission.

"Do I have hands on at the restaurant yet?"

"Within two minutes a team will be in place."

"Please, don't anyone stop this fool. Remember he's holding a hostage."

"Roger out."

Detective Hall placed the microphone down. He checked his watch again. He was anxious. *'Okay Doug, you're almost there. Don't panic.'*

Minutes later the restaurant came into view. Doug parked the unmarked sedan in the parking lot. He felt vulnerable because he had no idea of the facial recognition of the perpetrator. He continued onward. The restaurant was crowded with school kids on a field trip. Doug scanned the area. He saw customers at various tables eating and chatting. Doug done what was agreed upon by the perpetrator. He ordered a vanilla milkshake and a large order of french fries. He headed for a window seat in the mid-section of the restaurant. Looking for an empty table, Doug spotted a man sitting alone. He seemed to be in deep thought. He stared aimlessly out of the large pane glass window. Their eyes met. Suddenly, a woman with a small child exited the bathroom and joined him at the table. *That settles that.'*

Detective Hall found a seat as requested. He scanned the room for his handler but was unable to spot him. Suddenly, a man wearing a sports cap exited the men's room. He was wearing a denim outfit. He hurried into a seat at the opposite end of the table from Detective Hall.

Detective Hall was surprised. He would have never guess that the man in front of him to be the priest that he last saw. *'I must admit, his doctor has done an impressive job.'* He continued staring. "What is it that you want?"

Ralph reached over and took a french fry from Detective Hall's tray. "For beginners, I want 100 thousand dollars brought to the Mott Avenue subway station. The money is to be placed in a black, garbage bag and placed in a receptacle at the rear of the platform on the southbound side."

"Is that what this is all about? Money?"

"What else is there?"

"How and when do I get Dr Sutherland?"

Ralph reached into his pocket and handed the detective a cellphone. "I'll call you at three o'clock this evening when the cash is dropped. You will be notified where to pick her up." Ralph stood. "Remember, come alone or she's dead." Ralph began walking toward the exit. He passed the table with the family man with his wife and child. Simultaneously, the two collided into one another. The family man excused himself and patted the stranger on the back.

"Excuse me, I didn't see you passing. My mistake," said the family man.

Ralph saw the man was with his family. "That's all right. No harm done." He continued on his way. Ralph thought nothing of it. He exited the restaurant.

Doug sat smiling. The interception was splendid. It was expertly executed. He would have never guess the family man was the interceptor.

40

Ralph Sabian, aka Priest Carl Hamilton, headed back toward the train station from which he came. As he left the restaurant he smiled inwardly. *'That fool really thinks this is about money.'* A chuckled surfaced. *'Maybe that will keep him offset.'* He looked around to make sure he wasn't being followed. Feeling secure, he continued onward. Detective Hall and Dr Sutherland were insignificant to the scheme of things. He just wanted him out of the picture because of all his investigative quests. *'This time it will be phenomenal.'*

***

Doug watched the man that called himself Ralph Sabian exit the restaurant. It took every ounce of his fiber to restrain from attacking the perpetrator. He remained seated until he was out of sight. As far as Doug could tell, the perpetrator continued on foot down the street heading back toward Mott Avenue train station.

After a few moments, Doug spoke into his hand held radio. He looked around the restaurant as he talked.

"Com' on people! Tell me that you have eyes on him." He noticed that the family man remained in place. He understood the meaning behind it. In case other accomplices were on the premises he didn't want to be discovered.

"Roger, the eyes have the ball." The sound came from the radio. Static erupted between transmission.

"Okay, I'm going mobile. Roger out."

Doug drove his sedan on Beach Channel Drive listening to the reports from the dispatcher. Doug thought of the prior episode at the restaurant and smiled. The family man had placed an inconspicuous tracking device on Ralph Sabian's jacket when the two accidentally collided in the restaurant. That electronic device gave them the ability to keep a digital tab on their host.

"Talk to me people, where is he?"

"He appears to be adjacent to you on Beach Channel Drive. He's trailing on the northbound A-train. We're keeping tabs."

***

Ralph Sabian rode in the elevated A-train looking out the window at the tall, beige, brick buildings near the coastline. Overgrown grass and weeds took up a majority of the strip.

The stop that started his journey arrived but another notion came to his mind. He remained seated. He continued looking out of the window noticing the train began to descend from its elevated position toward the underground.

Twelve stops later, the train traveled in a subterranean. The train came to a halt at a station that held a large sign that read Rockaway Avenue. The station was located in the Brownsville section of Brooklyn. Ralph Sabian exited the train along with other commuters. The majority of the passengers were African-Americans.

Two blocks over on a street called Hopkinson Avenue, stood a building that was abandoned but under construction. He smiled as he entered the premises. A joyful emotion was felt as he looked around at the structure under construction. *This is going to be the ultimate masterpiece. But first, I have to get rid of the cop and his girl so that I can relax. No one has a clue that I'm going to control the outcome of humanity. It is I who was sent to lead the lost sheep.'*

***

Detective Hall raced down Atlantic Avenue to catch up with Carl. He picked up the two-way radio microphone. "Where is he now?"

The dispatcher high-pitched voice exploded in the vehicle. "He stopped at a location in Brownsville, Brooklyn. On Hopkinson

Avenue and Atlantic Avenue."

'Great! I"m not far from there.' He sighed. "Okay, nobody approach. Keep all uniform personnel and vehicles away. I don't want to spook him. Remember, he has a hostage." A few more blocks into the pursuit the dispatcher aired again.

"Perp is on the move again. An unmarked sedan has a fix on him. He's driving a black van and heading northbound on Atlantic Avenue. He should pass you within a block."

Doug kept his eyes plastered in the opposite lane. A vehicle stopped short in traffic, nearly causing him to ram into its rear. His car came to a screeching halt. Just then, the mentioned vehicle was passing in the opposite direction. "There you go!"

Detective Hall waited, giving the van a block distance. He used his siren and lights to make a quick U-turn. Quickly, he hurried in pursuit. He had no way of telling if Marlene was in the cargo compartment.

41

Detective Hall kept an inconspicuous distance behind the cargo van. He noticed it was heading toward Far Rockaway section of Queens. *'I wonder what he's up to?'* He picked up the two-way radio microphone. "It's almost time for the drop. I'm going to stay with him. That way if there is other players involved we'll still have a chance."

"Roger out." The transmission was terminated.

The cargo van drove southbound on Beach Channel Drive. 20 minutes later, it stopped in front of the old dilapidated house that held Marlene captive.

Ralph Sabian gazed around at his surroundings before entering. He stood in front of the house. Satisfied with the feeling of serenity the area provided, he headed inside.

The house reeked. A musky, stale, odor lingered in the air. Ralph headed for the bedroom. Dr Sutherland was unconscious from the drug that was administered to her as an inhalant. He stood over the bed to gaze at her. His perverted thoughts caused him to smile. Ralph walked toward the window and peered out. All seemed quiet. His attention was adverted to Marlene. She was adorned in hospital attire. He stood over her as she lie in bed.

"You my dear are so beautiful. I wonder what would happen if you were the host to conceive a child to the heir of the throne? To the magnificent empire that I am about to build." A sinister laugh followed. "Yes, I think there is time to find out." Ralph Sabian began disrobing at that very moment.

***

Detective Hall hid behind the building. There was tall grass all surrounding the structure. Discarded debris was strewn around the area. A malodorous stench permeated the air. The foul scent of decomposed animal carcasses was profound. Detective Hall began moving toward the house. He was thankful for the structure being a single family house. Otherwise, there would have been too many rooms to cover. His radio crackled. Detective Hall quickly turned it off. He wanted to call for backup but he didn't want to take any chances of spooking the priest. *I'm not even sure that Marlene is in here.'*

Stealthily, Doug made it to a rear window. His eyes focused on the interior. *'Damn it! It looks better on the outside.'* There was no movement inside. He tried to pry open the window but it wouldn't budge. Doug wanted to break the window but he knew it would draw unnecessary attention.

Making his way around toward the side of the house, another window came into view. He peered inside. It too was dirty and shabby. The room could have been used for a guest bedroom at its better days. The enclosure was absent of furniture, the only object inside was a mattress on the floor. The ceiling and walls were dingy and peeling. Detective Hall noticed parts of the walls and ceiling showed damp spots where roof rain seeped inside. Another area exposed the inner wall. Old wiring, studs, and cross members were visible.

Detective Hall tried the window. To his surprise it was unlocked. Quietly, he raised the window to gained access into the room. The bare wood floor was filthy. Detective Hall unholstered his weapon and inched forward on his tiptoes. He gave much effort to not give is position away. He knew the element of surprise was his only offense at the moment. He stopped to listen. All was quiet.

Ralph Sabian was stark naked. He mounted Dr Sutherland, who was also stripped bare. She was unconscious. He positioned her limp body with her legs wide apart. Ralph was instantly excited as he touched her soft, smooth, flawless skin. His pale member entered her cocoa complexion body. His sex organ was contrasted by the different hue. Ralph was fascinated by the concept. He couldn't remember the last time that he had sexual intercourse with the opposite sex. From his childhood to adulthood, he'd been confused about his sexuality.

Ralph Sabian's breathing began to deepen. He closed his eyes as he continued to thrust in and out of her warm, wet orifice. *'I will now bring forth the next generation to the throne.'* He began to shiver involuntarily from excitement. His body shuddered as his genetic fluids entered into Dr Sutherland's ovulating womb.

Oblivious to the external stimuli, Marlene was in a comatose state. As he reached the apex of his climax, Carl gave out an eerie yell.

Detective Hall inched forward. He came into the living room. Disappointment enveloped him as he saw it was unoccupied. Suddenly, a strange sound emitted from another part of the house. As quiet as possible, he registered a round into the chamber of his Colt .45 caliber, semi-automatic handgun. A metallic sound of steel hitting steel seemed louder than it actually was.

Doug followed the sound. He neared a door. He could hear activity going on the other side of the closed door. He placed his ear to the wooden partition. The sounds became audible. He silently tried turning the doorknob. To his surprise it turned freely. There was no keyhole to see the activity on the other side.

Detective Hall took in a deep breath. As he exhaled, he pushed open he door forcefully with his weapon drawn. Using his training, he quickly scanned the room as he access the situation. His eyes dilated as he took in the scene. His brain took moments longer to process what he was witnessing.

Totally surprised, Ralph turned toward him. Their eyes were now locked on one another. Doug let off two sharp staccato blasts from his weapon. Loud, thunderous noise exploded in the room. It was followed by bright light as fire expelled from the muzzle of Detective Hall's weapon. A pungent scent followed. It was the tell-tale of cordite being discharge. The emotional display on Ralph's face proved he was totally surprised. The projectiles emitted from the weapon forcefully hitting the intended target. A tiny hole was in Ralph's forehead, and another in his throat. The exit wounds were more severe as bone fragments, blood, and membranes splattered the area behind him. He fell dead at the foot of Marlene's unconscious body.

Doug wasted no time. He hurried over to Marlene. For a moment he thought the worst. He checked for vitals. A smile ensued when he found a pulse. She was breathing faintly. At that moment the room began to fill with police and emergency workers.

ONE

MONTH

LATER

42

SAINT LUTHERAN HOSPITAL
BROOKLYN, NEW YORK
10:27 AM

Detective Hall impatiently paced back and forth in the waiting area. After the ordeal, Marlene had undergone multiple tests. Some physical, some psychological. Marlene had no recollection of the past events. After being given the facts about the case, she was traumatized. Her mood had become sullen. She didn't express interest in her work as she'd done in the past. She showed no enthusiasm to adventure outdoors much. The greatest obstacles that she was faced with was being impregnated during the ordeal. Normally, the procedure would be simple, to abort the pregnancy, but Marlene's reproduction system was unfit to receive that sort of treatment. This was due to the enlargement of the fallopian tube linings. Any pressure could kill her. It was a risk either way. With the act of aborting the pregnancy or in conception. She was going through a stage by stage observation to see what could be done.

Doug stopped his pacing when he saw Marlene exit from the doctor's office. She headed toward his direction. He tried to read her expression as she approached. The two embraced. Doug was totally into Marlene. He truly loved her. It didn't matter to him whatsoever she decided as long as they were together. That was all that mattered to him. He tried to read her expression as she approached. The two embraced. He carried his love for her on the surface for everyone to see. Marlene surrendered to his request and fell in love also.

"Well? Is there anything different to report than what we already know? asked Doug. He held Marlene close as he gazed into her brown eyes.

"They said time is of an essence because soon I will not be able to abort…" Her voice crackled as she tried to control her emotion. "Doug, I'm scared."

Doug squeezed her hands firmly. "Don't be. Whatever you decide I am with you 100 percent."

I understand, but it feels like a catch 22. Damn if I don't, damn if I do."

"Did they give you any percentages?"

"The higher percentage is to go through full term with the pregnancy." Tears flowed down her cheeks.

Doug held her steadily. "Com' on, let's get you home."

***

Marlene busied herself making a nutritious lunch. Doug sat at the kitchen table while Marlene, dressed in a floral pattern apron, prepared the food. The two conversed.

"Marlene, I want to show you something." Doug reached into his pocket and produced a document.

Marlene wiped her hands on a towel attached to the apron as she headed toward the table. "What is that?" She took a seat next to Doug.

"Read it." He handed the document to her.

Marlene gazed at Doug feeling bewildered. "When did you decide to do this?"

Doug sipped on a glass of orange juice. "The moment I met you. It became final after the ordeal with you and finding the murderer to the orphan I searched so long for. You remember I told you about it. Everything feels like a sign. You are a new chapter in my life."

"Okay, you've resigned. Now what?"

"I found a nice house on the market up in Yonkers, New York. I figured…" Doug reached into his pocket and produced a black, velvet case. He opened it to expose a brilliant four carat diamond ring that equivocally matched the engagement ring that he'd given to her earlier on. "That you would move into it as my wife."

Tears of endearment filled down her cheeks. Everything was happening so quickly. Marlene looked at the ring, then at Doug. Emotionally, she was overwhelmed. She stood and raced from the room.

Doug was empathetic to her reaction. *'Maybe it's bad timing on my part. I'm such a klutz.'* He smacked himself on the head. Doug went after her.

Knocking softly on the bedroom door, Doug talked from the hall. "Please, Marlene I didn't mean to make you feel sad. I only want the best for you. I love you with all my heart. Whatever you're going through I want to make it my problem also. When we solve it, you will know we've done it together. All I want to do is share the earth with you. You make me…" The door opened abruptly to a giggling Marlene.

"Come inside silly." She moved aside to allow Doug entrance. Marlene held him near. "I'm not sadden by your gesture, just upset. Here sit down." Doug sat on the edge of he queen-size bed. Marlene joined him. "Do you realize I am carrying another man's child? Where does that leave us?"

"I'm trying to show you. Marlene it doesn't matter. I want to be with you. The child is an innocent being. There's no way to use that as a wedge between us because there's none."

"I love you Doug Hall."

"Then will you become Mrs Hall?"

Marlene smiled. She forgot about the turmoil that she had felt. "Yes, I would love to be your wife." The two embraced and kissed. They stared into one another's eyes. "Com' on, the food is getting cold."

TWO

YEARS

LATER

43

Marlene exited her vehicle in the garage of her new home in Yonkers, New York. They were located in a well kept neighborhood with tree lined streets and admirably beautiful landscaped yards. The house, an Old Victorian-styled home, was a sight to behold. The exterior was constructed with large bay windows and old fashion shutters. The other homes in the neighborhood were spaced apart. It gave the atmosphere an airy, pleasant ambiance.

Marlene's arms were filled with groceries. She headed up the steps to the porch area. She fumbled around for her keys. She had to switch the packages around in her grasp. She finally completed her tasked and entered the house to the joyous sounds of her family.

Doug was on the carpeted floor holding and tickling his newborn son who was now sixteen months old. The cooing sounds brought laughter from the newborn.

"Hey, I'm home. What are you guys up to?" asked Marlene.

"Oh? Just showing Isaiah who's boss." Doug chuckled. "How was your day at work?"

"Not bad, I had only two surgeries to perform today. Both of them went well."

Doug placed his son in his bassinet. "Here, let me help you with the groceries. Did you remember to get my vanilla Swiss almond ice cream?"

Marlene smiled and nodded. "Yes, I've not forgotten your ice cream," she mimicked.

Doug relieved her of the grocery bags. Marlene headed for the bassinet to pick up her son.

"Boy, I miss you. Wow! You're getting heavier by the second." She stared at her son. Marlene turned her attention toward Doug, who was now in the kitchen. "Honey, if we don't watch his weight we'll have to get a wheelbarrow to move him around in." She stared at her son Isaiah. "Ain't that right snookie?" She kissed him on the cheek. The gesture brought more giggles. It was as if he understood what she was saying.

Placing him back in his bassinet, she began taking off her jacket. Marlene rolled the bassinet into the kitchen so that she could keep a watchful eye on him.

The sounds of the paper grocery bags crinkled in the room as Doug filled the refrigerator and stocked the shelves. "Why so much food?"

"Well, I told my friends I'll have them over for dinner. Afterward, you can go out and have fun. You deserve it." She gave him a wink.

After the baby arrived, Doug was the perfect husband. He was caring and attentive to all of Marlene's needs. She was so thrilled with the way he took over the responsibilities for everything. From the first day home, he treated Isaiah as if he were the biological father.

Isaiah was a light tan complexion boy with hazel eyes and reddish hair. Marlene's dominant genes were woven into his facial appearance. His smooth complexion, almond shaped eyes, small lips, and round nose exposed his African heritage.

Doug never mentioned anything to her about it. As far as she was concerned it was his first child. He had planned on having more and she was willing.

EPILOGUE

Isaiah Hall was growing to be a strong, wonderful boy. The little girls in his circle were intrigued by his distinctive facial features. He was polite and cheerful. At age eight he was in school, attending his third grade class.

The room was noisy with children talking while seated in rows in the modest-size classroom. The teacher was at the blackboard writing the day's lesson. Finished, she turned around.

"Okay class, that's enough. Pay attention." The group of children began to settle down to her command.

Isaiah was sitting in the rear of the classroom quiet. He was preoccupied with doodling in his notebook. It had become a pastime for him. If anyone would have given it any notice, they would have been alarmed at the drawings and writings.

"Okay class, on the blackboard I have written different occupations for you to choose from. Now don't be troubled if something you like isn't on the blackboard. Say it anyway and I'll add it to the list of jobs. Let's start with you Terry. Don't forget you have to say why is it you've chosen a particular career."

Terry was a small boy with blonde hair and freckles. He wore thick eyeglasses. He stood facing the teacher. "I would like to be an engineer. I chose that career because it is what my father does. He is able to help us live in a big house and have nice things." He sat back down.

"Very nicely said Terry. Okay, who's next?" The teacher, Miss Blanchard, was a young shapely teacher on her third year tenure at the elementary school. She scanned the room noticing all the hands that were raised. The eagerness to be heard was encouraging to her. She continued her observation. Her focus was in the rear of the room. "Isaiah Hall. Why don't you stand up and tell the class what it is that you would like to do?"

All eyes focused on Isaiah. He stood reluctantly. "I would like to be a priest. I chose that because I like to read the Bible, and I feel that it is my mission to save and lead the sheep to the promise land. I don't know why. It's just in me to do." He sat down.

The class was quiet. Miss Blanchard was taken aback by his choice of profession at such an early age. She regained control of the class.

"Okay class, let's face front. That was very good Isaiah. I will add that to the blackboard."

Isaiah resumed his activity in his notebook. He drew pictures of crosses with blood dripping down the sides of it. He had written passages from the bible's Revelation chapter. The passages were exact quotes from the book, word for word. The strange things was that he'd never read the book. In reality, he had never read anything past children stories. A thought struck him. A sinister smile followed.